Elizabeth Tan (@ElzbthT) is a Perth writer and sessional academic at Curtin University. Her first book of fiction, *Rubik*, was published in 2017, and went on to be published in North America (The Unnamed Press) and the United Kingdom (Wundor Editions). She was the co-editor of the 2019 anthology *In This Desert, There Were Seeds*, a collaboration between Margaret River Press of Western Australia and Ethos Books of Singapore. *Smart Ovens For Lonely People* is Elizabeth's second book.

BRIO

First published by Brio in 2020
Reprinted in 2020

Brio Books
PO Box Q324, QVB Post Office,
NSW 1230, Australia
www.briobooks.com.au

978-1-922267-19-1 (print)
978-1-922267-20-7 (digital)

Text copyright © Elizabeth Tan 2020
Cover and internal design and typesetting copyright © Brio Books Pty Ltd 2020
Cataloguing-in-publication data is available from the National Library of Australia

Cover and internal design by Brio
Printed and bound by McPherson's Printing Group

SMART OVENS FOR LONELY PEOPLE

ELIZABETH TAN

b

BRIO

CONTENTS

NIGHT OF THE FISH

The slide was always too hot in the summertime. There was no way you could smoothly descend—your sweat would fasten your thighs to the plastic; you'd squeak all the way down. This one summer, Josh Perkins got in trouble for holding his little brother's face to the slide at midday when it was forty out—little Dylan had mouthed off to Josh, or dobbed on him for taking an extra Zooper Dooper from the freezer—and the scorched red mark on Dylan's cheek didn't fade for days. On some afternoons you might've found one of the neighbourhood cats curled up at the base of the slide, absorbing the last of the day's warmth—sometimes the boys would go down the slide on purpose and send the cat flailing into the sandpit. At the top of the slide there was a little pointed roof which was painted to resemble the head of a fish. There were overlapping rainbow-coloured circles for the fish's scales, two saucer eyes, and thick fat lips at the roof's apex.

On the night it happened, Cassie and I were sleeping on the floor of the living room with the ceiling fan on. An aching groan rumbled through our street, lifted us clean out of our dreams. We sat up on our knees, swept the curtain aside: the fish was out there in the street, teetering on stilt legs, the slide barely tethered to its head. It lurched and swayed like a broken circus tent, ready to topple at any moment; with each step it moaned like a whale or a slack-stringed cello—such deep, long, agonising notes. As the fish passed by our house, its slide swung out and decapitated the letterbox.

I felt pee trickling down my leg but I managed to stop when Cassie put her arms around me and said it was okay, the fish wouldn't come for us. And it didn't come for us—or anybody—not even Josh Perkins, who, as Dylan would glee-fully recall the next day, wet himself so much that their mum had to change his bedspread.

The council never replaced the slide. In fact, they tore the whole playground down, poured concrete into the sandpit, installed a picnic table. Said the play equipment was old, said it wasn't up to code—but I reckon they were actually scared. Scared that the playground was sentient, livelier than they could possibly imagine. Grown-ups had a way of doing that—flattening their fears with concrete, building something neat and pretty on top, as if life really were a picnic.

OUR SLEEPING LUNGS OPENED TO THE COLD

They didn't know that we had changed. When they created us, they named us for precious stones—Sapphire, Opal, Ruby, Jade. We were created for adoration, indexed behind glass. We were created sleek, glowing, hair lustrous as hallucinations; our tails gleamed as if each scale had been lacquered by hand; we were created graceful and ripe—Diamond, Garnet, Emerald, Pearl. When the restaurant was open we swirled behind the glass walls, floating spectacles for the tables of dignitaries, well-heeled couples, high-rollers giddy with luck well spent; we spun languid corkscrews through the shining water. At night when the customers were gone, when the last waiter would hang up his apron or the chef his white hat, we would sink to the bottom of the aquarium and sleep with limbs and tails entangled, a fluttering octet, our breath vibrating through ourselves and each other and the water, meeting the hum of the purifier in a somnolent fugue.

The adjustment was only incremental—a reduction in the chemical that kept us docile, to accommodate the fish they released into the aquarium. It did make for a more striking display, having other aquatic life to complement our beauty; it brought new wonder to the eyes of the clientele, deepened their love. They would order another glass of wine, and then another, mesmerised; the restaurant's opening hours stretched into the early morning. A photograph of Ruby with yellow tangs nestled in her billowing hair made the cover of *National Geographic*, and the restaurant was fully booked for the next six months.

We believe that the aquarist truly loved us. He would visit us once a week with his wooden box that unfolded on zigzag hinges, kneeling beside the hatch to collect a trembling sample of water in his vial. On rare occasions, he would arrive in a black, oily skin with ungainly flippers and breathing apparatus—would plunge into the tank, scrape algae or calcium from the rocks for testing. Only a few of us ever witnessed this ritual directly—Sapphire was the first to have seen him do it—because they would increase the dosage of the sedating chemical each time this testing was necessary. In fact, any time there was some drastic change to the aquarium—the last of which was the introduction of the fish—we would be lulled to sleep by the sedative slipping invisibly between our gills. The aquarist never touched us, but we loved him.

We all dreamt about the aquarist. Garnet described one dream in which the aquarist stood for a long time at the edge of the hatch—not in his vulgar skin-tight suit and flippers, but in his regular trousers and navy-blue shirt with the cuffs folded up to the elbows. He knelt to untie his shoelaces and pull his shoes from his feet, and then his socks. Garnet admired but did not envy his toes, flexible stumps of coral, crenelated like teeth. Last of all he took off his spectacles and folded them next to his shoes—and then, with this final piece of glass between them removed, he slipped into the water. For all his gracelessness, he was beautiful: arms hovering, toes pointed, dancer-like, to the aquarium floor. Garnet swam to him. He was warm, she said. A man-shaped membranous sac of blood.

Later, we would conclude that the aquarist didn't foresee the cumulative effects of reducing the sedative.

We started eating the smallest fish first—the damsels, gobies, blennies. We liked to feel them darting, wriggling in the caves of our mouths, before we swallowed them whole. Then the larger fish—the angels and basses—where Emerald discovered the pleasure of fine bone snapping under teeth. We would wait until the customers were gone and plot which fish to take next, to pass between us and feast upon, their slippery flesh and jellied eyes, scales flaking from skin, meat peeled from the vertebral column. We always marvelled at the way their blood disappeared so quickly in the water, assimilated into benign clarity.

Our bodies were not so fragile: they thickened in glory.

Collarbones sank beneath the luxurious swell of flesh. We liked the way the water held us, our new presence within it; we were increasing in corporeality and palpability, more vowel than consonant; we became orchestras. Our scales, which formerly terminated at our hips, began to multiply on our waists, then our stomachs, then our breasts, then our arms. The webbing between our fingers slid closer to the tips; our pupils fattened while our eyelids receded.

The customers did not enjoy our transformations as much as we did—there was a dissonant modulation in their stares, a curdling of the irises—but, as we grew, life outside the aquarium shrank in importance, inconsequential as the blood of our prey. What delighted us was each other, our turning into something less hollow. We no longer adhered to the rhythms of the restaurant, the customers' comings and goings—if we desired sleep, we slept; if we desired privacy, we retreated to the furthest reaches of the aquarium, huddled in molluscular indifference.

When we did stare outwards, it was deliberate, silent. We liked to lock eyes with a customer about to eat; we liked to watch for the quivering pause of the fork to the mouth.

By the time the proprietors increased the frequency of the aquarist's visits, it was too late. Most of us had developed scales up to our chins; Diamond's scales encased her head almost completely. We were arcing towards our metamorphic conclusion, following the imperative of our blood and bodies. We could pull our hair in fistfuls from our scalps; the untethered strands would float away like undulating harp notes. On the surface, the hair would be less magical, gathering thickly near the hatch, where the aquarist would be waiting with his zip-lock bags. Eventually the sight of us would become so unnerving to the customers that the restaurant was forced into what was soberly reported as—and what the proprietors handwringingly hoped would be—a temporary closure.

At first we wondered: What was it about us that disturbed the clients so thoroughly? But then Opal refracted the question: What was it about us that they so loved to begin with?

In those final days when the restaurant was closed, the aquarist was our only visitor. He'd created a makeshift lab in one of the plush booths, testing sample after sample, as if the nutrients in the water would take pity—would join cells to spell out for him an unambiguous resolution on the microscope slide. The aquarist refused to follow the proprietors' suggestion to sedate us—he didn't want to harm the fish—and it is this kindness, this devotion to the living, that permitted our migration.

We needed to escape while we still had arms. The restaurant was embedded in the casino complex, and had no outward-facing windows. And yet we could hear the storm, like a baby in the womb might hear the voice of her mother, and the voice said: This is the time.

Jade had been the last to see the aquarist operate the hatch door from the inside. One by one we clambered out, those still in the water helping to hoist the climber. On the gangplank our gills collapsed; we breathed for the first time with mouth and lung, overwhelmed with sensation, the strangest of which was *wetness*, for surely we had always been wet, but separate from our habitual context our dampness acquired some more pungent meaning. The sound of us grappling for oxygen supplanted the throb of the purifier as our pulse; we were all at once irregular, out of time, cold and trembling and porous.

Transplanted from the water, our bodies lost fluency; we fumbled with elbows bent amphibian-wise. Our skin opened from the clamour of new textures, from the metal grid of the gangplank to the carpet of the restaurant to the marble tiles of the grand foyer; we left a painful trail of blood and hair and chipped scales. We crawled, clustered as close as possible in our octet, allowing the fatigued ones to crest for a time on the ones who could move, sliding over and around each other in a reinvention of our former effortless flight.

We couldn't say if we truly expected to survive. We were only following the sound of the storm, the churning of rain; we were making an offering of faith to our morphing bodies. We expected more resistance, but the casino patrons we encountered recoiled from us, fleeing from our path as if we were carriers of some evolutionary glitch, our scuffling forms neither fish nor human nor mermaid.

We toppled into the storm, still clutching together in our octet, into the rain's brutal percussion; the streets were slick and dark like the aquarist's diving suit, the moon a shucked oyster. There was a place where the rain struck an expanse of water, we were sure of it; we were sobbing—another new sensation—heaving our tails across the bicycle path, the soaked grass, the embankment of rocks.

We don't know which one of us entered the water first: perhaps we tumbled into our new home knotted and united, blooming in the re-found weightlessness. Or: perhaps we lost consciousness on the rocks, and the river's oscillations, in their slow, benevolent way, coaxed us into its embrace. Parted our gills, arches flexing like cathedrals.

Where we are now, the light comes from above—we must crane our necks to look outside ourselves; we must break the surface to see clearly. Where we are now, there is such a surface to break. Where we are now, we are not observed, or exalted, or feared: we glide and somersault and feast; the bubbles of our breath drift skyward like arpeggios. In this water, soupy and fecund, there is no vigilant metronome of the purifier, no crosshatch of gazes, no glass vertices. This gentle darkness, this soft temple. This loving body, unspooling from the harness of man-made meaning.

A GIRL IS SITTING ON A UNICORN IN THE MIDDLE OF A SHOPPING CENTRE

It's Monday and Myer is having the greatest stocktake sale of all time, and there's a giant backlit poster of Miranda Kerr smiling indulgently with a wrist of pearls, and the shopping centre is flooded with daylight and hope. There is a girl sitting on a unicorn in the middle of the shopping centre and the artificial trees are green and shimmering and the lady at the make-up counter waits with an armful of flyers and a cherry-flavoured smile. It's Monday and children tug their parents' sleeves and ask if they can ride the pony or the zebra or the tiger; they clamber into miniature saddles and pedal the giant animals across the chequered tiles. There is a girl sitting on a unicorn in the middle of the shopping centre, framed in the square of a skylight, wearing jelly sandals and pink tights and a tutu skirt and a T-shirt which says 'Elsa & Anna'.

It's Monday and today there are specials like no other and there are pert macarons at the patisserie counter that are all the colours of a chalky rainbow. There are vast pyramids of cruelty-free bath bombs that smell like avocado or honey or fizzy sherbet. Miranda Kerr is smiling and her teeth are brighter than a cache of luxury steak knives and her eyes are huge caverns of feeling. She believes in her pearl bracelet and she wants you to believe that she believes in her pearl bracelet and together you have a special understanding, just you and Miranda Kerr and nobody else.

It's Monday and there are unbelievable markdowns and shoppers mill around with their arms crossed waiting for their Boost Juice. There is a girl sitting on a unicorn in the middle of the shopping centre, concentrating fiercely; one hand grips the decorative reins and the other hand is buried in the knotted purple fibres of the unicorn's mane. This unicorn has been the chosen mount of forty-three children before this girl. This girl is the last hope.

If you go into Woolworths there is a man in a novelty chef's hat and butcher's apron handing out little medicine cups of toothpick-pierced grilled chicken in a spiced, creamy sauce. A shopper tries to request Cash Out from a self-serve check-out machine that does not offer Cash Out, and there are no more cone-shaped bags at the buckets of flowers, so anybody who takes a bunch of flowers gets a little bit wet. At the deli counter, carved slices of ham are precisely layered on a slight incline, and each pink face is a round gleaming universe.

There is a girl sitting on a unicorn in a square of light. She is listening to the unicorn intently. She has unthreaded her feet from the pedal-stirrups and she is listening most, most carefully. She is a good listener. Oftentimes, instead of telling the girl to be quiet, the girl's mother will give the tips of her ears a very gentle push forward and say, 'Use your listening ears for now, please.' Her mother, Elsa, and Anna are the girl's most favourite people in the world.

It's Monday and the shopping centre is filled with children's laughter and avian and rainforest sounds courtesy of the Australian Geographic store, and the girl leans close to the unicorn and shuts her eyes and nuzzles its furry head. She is using her listening ears. The unicorn says that it doesn't know how it can go on. The unicorn says that it wants to die.

Miranda Kerr smiles and her cheeks are round pink gleaming universes, especially her left one, and the more you stare at her the more you understand the truth of reality. A spotless shopfront window displays a grid of sneakers separated from their right halves. All the sneakers are facing in the same direction, showing off their optimal side, just like Miranda. The pearl bracelet and Miranda Kerr have mutually enhancing special powers and Miranda Kerr's hair is imbued with several compelling subliminal messages like *a rich aromatic blend* and *melted to the finest consistency* and *a soft comfortable lining with the firmest support suitable for everyday wear.*

The girl strokes the unicorn's hair and the unicorn corrects itself and says that it doesn't want to die exactly but that it just wants to stop, like this: 'One day, the unicorn stopped.' And all the beautiful things of the world would still be there and all the sad things of the world would still be there and the unicorn can just be quiet and disconnected and not even be an 'it' anymore. I cannot turn off the voice inside my head that is telling me it wants to stop, the unicorn says.

The girl can feel her breakfast inside her stomach, warm and milky, and she doesn't need to pee just yet, and she doesn't know it, and will never know it, but she is a miracle. She wears her tutu skirt and jelly sandals and she thinks she would like to pierce her ears one day and she loves her mum and Elsa and Anna and she will never be ashamed of any of this. It pleases her to be a girl and to be like other girls because the best people in her life are all girls, so why wouldn't she want to be like other girls?

Everything in the girl's life is small and satisfying but she listens to the unicorn and hugs its neck and says that it's okay to be sad and it's okay to feel like you would like to stop. And she rubs her nose in the unicorn's mane and smells the dyed fibres and the noses of the forty-three children who have ridden this unicorn before her. She is sad that the unicorn is sad and together they sit in the square of light and give each other the best of their attention.

At PappaRich a waiter carries a stack of clean white dishes which is so high it reaches his chin. There are squat amber bottles filled with tap water lined up on a counter and throughout the restaurant bells are always chiming. The faceless mannequins in the Portmans window are all naked except for giant red price tags hanging around each of their necks, which say SALE. A boy guides a zebra back to the smiling vendor. A shop assistant slides a dress into a crisp new bag.

It's Monday and you do not want to miss out on these never-before-seen limited-time offers. There is a girl sitting on a unicorn in the middle of the shopping centre. Miranda Kerr is listening to every word you are saying and she can even see your thoughts. The shopping centre smells aggressively of salted caramel courtesy of Peter Alexander, but if you use your smelling nose you might also catch the scent of clothing tags and unworn leather and slightly burned coffee and steamed kaya buns and boneless easy-carve pork roasts and artisan baguettes and perfume samples and moisturising self-foaming hand wash and orange rinds.

The unicorn and the girl sit in the square of light and together they build a special understanding that will last until the end of time. One day the girl will stop and the unicorn will stop and Miranda Kerr will stop and the shopping centre will stop and the light will stop and the pyramids of cruelty-free bath bombs will crumble into nothing. One day there will be a sale to end all sales, a final markdown like a lightning strike that tears the sky in half. And all the beautiful things of the world will still be there and all the sad things of the world will still be there. And all the glass and skylights will melt down into a universe of the finest consistency—round, pink, gleaming. A place so quiet and small and satisfying. It's Monday, and all the bells are chiming.

PANG & CO. GENUINE SCRIBE ERA STATIONERY PTY LTD

She was the daughter of a pencil salesman. Her youth was cluttered with obsolescent toys—stencils, felt-tip markers. She inherited not only her father's love of stationery, but an entire shop of such relics, on the corner of Croft and Milton. Everything there is expensive and exquisite, and the place is quiet as a museum. It is with perfunctory satisfaction that Ira Pang locks her store on this afternoon, a winter Thursday, while the billboards change their colours to complement the night.

Kit meets her at the restaurant with his cuffs unbuttoned and tie relaxed. The company has given him a new phone and now she must admire it. He says, 'It's just a prototype. The alarm clock releases smells to wake you up.' She points out that this technology was developed a very long time ago, and Kit says, 'Yes, but this time it's on my *phone*.'

Kit is also expensive and exquisite. He is as smooth and impressive as a skyscraper, and she expects that if she were to shrink herself and walk inside him she would find his insides similarly straightened, the blood flowing along escalators, his memories alphabetised in cabinets and backed up in a data warehouse. He keeps his spectacles and sunglasses in separate cases. If he were stranded on a deserted island he would either vaporise or create a sustainable economy in two weeks.

The waiter arrives with their food, and Kit slips his phone away. 'The new Icebreakers campaign is debuting on the billboard on Croft Street later tonight, right near your store,' he says. 'I don't suppose you'd be terribly interested in coming to see it with me.'

She looks out of the restaurant's tall glass windows. It will be cold, but the walk to Croft Street is a short one. 'Of course,' she says.

After dinner they retrace her steps back to Croft Street and stand in the billboard's oblong glow, craning their necks, waiting for Kit's advertisement to come on. The picture for Icebreaker peppermints is an assertive white against the night sky. Kit has brought home samples of the confectionery before. Each mint is individually wrapped—a risky move in the face of Icebreaker's more quickly dispensed competitors— but upon unwrapping the mint, the consumer reveals a tiny fact imprinted on the waxed paper.

The expression 'stamp of approval' refers to a rubber mould, covered in ink and then 'stamped' on the physical page, leaving an impression behind.

The 'rewind' symbol on a music player is the same used on cassette players, in which tape is literally 'rewound' so that it can be played again.

The QWERTY keyboard layout was originally designed to spread out the more commonly used letters of the alphabet to prevent jams in typewriters.

Each of these facts, Ira realises now, relates to some redundant element of technology that persists to the present day. Kit has created a new slogan for Icebreakers, which appears in cursive writing now: *Some things never go out of style.* These mints are not meant to be hurriedly choked down before a job interview or first date: they are conversation starters; they are meant to be offered and shared between overscheduled unscruffy white collar consumers, like the couple on the billboard now, at some kind of in-between-meetings lunch, holding their flattened wrappers and smiling at their tiny facts. Kit has differentiated the homogenous, has created a new market—for *breath mints*. She hardly knows what to say in the face of such calculated cleverness.

The advertisement fades away, and for a moment, so does the white oblong in which they stand. 'So where's my Icebreaker?' she asks him, but Kit is already pressing an Icebreaker into her hand.

'Use it wisely.'

The billboard has moved on to a new advertisement, so

they begin walking back to the apartment.

It is on the deserted stretch of Gibson Avenue that they encounter the homeless man. 'Got a sandwich?' he asks, and Ira quite suddenly can't recall the last time she has seen a homeless person, as if the city is so clean and smooth that men like him are instantly tweezed out.

The man is standing directly in their path. Kit chews the inside of his cheek. 'I'm sorry,' he says. 'I don't have anything for you.'

'I see,' the man says. If his odour had a colour, it would be the worn, decaying yellow of an old book.

'Here,' Ira says, as quickly as her hand can dive into her pocket and grasp the first thing it touches. It's a biro from work, with a click-top and scratchy blue ink. It's not exactly a rare treasure but perhaps he can trade it at an antique dealership for the price of a meal. She holds it out to the man. Kit watches.

The man closes his hand around the pen. His eyes do not change, and, Ira supposes, neither will his fortune. The pen leaves her grasp and she is suddenly worried that this will not placate him, but his hand drops by his side. He thumbs the click-top.

Kit nods. 'Good evening.'

He takes Ira's hand and they walk. They round the corner, take twenty paces, and come to the steps of their apartment block. The encounter reverberates like a dream.

Ira stares down at her fingers. 'Should we call somebody?' she asks.

Kit glances up the street. 'No, he'll be fine,' he says, and she is too ashamed to admit that she had meant to report him.

Inside the apartment, Kit slings off his tie while Ira plucks out her earrings and places them in a bowl on their bedside table. She goes to the bathroom to wash her face, and wonders what it is like to be hungry for days and days.

Overnight, while Ira and Kit hold hands even in sleep, blue scratches grow on the walls of the subway tunnels; agitated, thin, stirring like mosquitoes charged on blood and light and singular purpose, and in the morning, a homeless man throws himself under Friday's first train.

The story stops her in the middle of breakfast. It's all happening live, the reporter taking her through the subway, panning across the frenetic blue scratches. Kit's new Infinity Pixel monitor is finally proving its worth, because the blue is sharper than perception itself, a more intense and urgent blue than Ira remembers the pen capable of producing. Most of it is illegible and erratic, like polygraph needle scrawls, but occasionally she can make out a quaking word that the homeless man had copied from surrounding advertisements.

Ira is quite suddenly grateful that Kit has already gone to work, that she doesn't have to talk to him about the news while she doesn't yet know the word for what she feels. But a conversation about this is inevitable and she is sure Kit already knows, and is thinking of her at this moment. He takes the train to work: even if he doesn't travel on that part of the subway he will surely note the slightest delay in his commute and wonder; and even if *that* doesn't tip him off, his new phone probably sent him an alert about it, probably told him the story of the homeless man's death before she even poured her glass of orange juice.

They show the tracks now—not the place where he died, but the raw streaks left by the train's brakes. They show the wrecked windshield of the train; they talk to an I-saw-the-whole-thing bystander who presumably doesn't have to be at work this morning, telling what the astute viewer might have already inferred: *There was a bang and the sound of something dragged along the tracks, and then there was just this screeching, screeching like my ex-wife, ha-ha-ha.*

They return, again, to the blue scratches. It is the only thing making this event exceptional enough for the news to cover. They show security footage of the homeless man in a time lapse, so he is at moments squatting, stretching, sitting, but all the time clutching the biro in his fist. They suggest that he was ill. Some interviewees bravely speculate that the homeless man was a kind of seer, and the scribbles contain clues to the end of the world. They show a commuter wearing a red beanie as he trails in front of the wall, his phone flipped open and recording. A historian older than the city itself talks about graffiti and tagging and they dredge up archival footage from the earliest days of the twenty-first century. Everybody expresses surprise that the pen didn't run out of ink.

The climax of the segment is the paramedics wheeling the body bag into the glass elevator and ascending to the reporter's sign-off.

When it is over, Ira stands in the kitchen with a half-glass of orange juice she doesn't want to drink. The mere fact of her aliveness makes her feel too guilty to pour it down the drain. She puts the glass in the fridge and goes to work.

Not one of the customers that drift into her store that day purchases a biro. It's as if the biro has become a talisman for destruction and madness.

It is four o'clock when the police investigators arrive. She has been expecting *something* to happen, so when they stride through the door it is a peculiar relief. She endures their introductions with a kind of itchy impatience, as if those blue scribbles are inside her, evolving into something parasitic.

Finally: 'I suppose you've seen the news this morning, about the man on the subway?'

'Yes. I did.'

The one called Langford takes out a plastic zip-lock bag with the biro inside. She recognises the zip-lock bag: two years ago Kit was always having meetings for it, pitching concept after concept. All along, they should have been targeting crime scene investigators.

It is with the greatest concentration that she looks at the biro. 'Yours is the only stationery dealership in the city,' Langford says, 'that still sells Bic pens.'

'That's right.'

'This pen was found with the body.'

'I'm so sorry.'

The investigators look at each other and Ira knows that she has said the wrong thing, although it is exactly what she is feeling. 'You're … not in trouble, Ms Pang,' Langford says. 'Please don't be alarmed by our questions. Did you see Mr Carroll on the night before his death?'

His name is like a stone in her stomach. If the news report had mentioned it, she certainly didn't catch it. 'My partner and I were walking home from dinner. We saw him on Gibson Avenue. He asked us for food. I only had this pen, so I gave it to him. And then we walked away.'

All this time, the other investigator is taking notes on his phone. Ira wonders what kind of sensible applications a police investigator would have on his phone, and imagines that any of them would be more useful than a scented alarm clock.

'It must have been very distressing to hear the news this morning, then,' Langford says.

'Yes. I suppose it was.'

'Would you like the name of a counsellor, Ms Pang? Would you like to talk to somebody?'

'No.' She thinks for a while. 'No, I'm only sorry that it didn't turn out well for Mr Carroll.'

Langford nods. He puts the biro back into the zip-lock bag then into his pocket. The other investigator has stopped taking notes: he is admiring a leather-bound organiser next to the counter. He smiles at Ira. 'My father always used one of these, right up until he died a few years ago. Even when they started getting hideously expensive.'

'It has a different feel, doesn't it,' she says, 'to have all your days spread out like that.'

He levels his hand on the cover. 'I think I'll buy one.'

Langford snorts. 'Aw come on, Jordan. You're not really going to use it.'

'I *will*. It looks fun.'

'You don't own a pen. I haven't seen you use a pen in the entire time I've known you.'

Jordan laughs. 'Well I'll *buy* one!'

'Let me give you one,' Ira says, her hand diving into her pocket. Her fingers brush against the Icebreaker from the night before, lying in wait like Chekhov's gun. Ira wonders why she didn't give Mr Carroll the mint instead.

She quickly retracts her hand, takes a pen from the basket on the counter and presents it to Jordan.

The organiser costs $74.90. Ira packs it in a paper bag, which Jordan carries as fondly as a photograph. As they leave, Ira takes out the Icebreaker from her pocket and unwraps it. She chews the mint slowly and uncreases her tiny fact:

A single Scribe Era ballpoint pen, 14 cm in length, could produce up to a kilometre of ink.

'I think the news reports were right about one thing,' Kit says. 'He wasn't in good shape when we saw him. He was probably very unwell. He probably hadn't eaten for days or even weeks.'

They're at the restaurant where each table has a communal hotpot of soup, to which the diners add meat and vegetables of their choice. Ira is relieved to be at this restaurant, to not have to interact with the waitstaff for too long.

'It's sad,' Kit says. 'I felt sad when I found out.' He contemplates his empty bowl. 'Didn't you?'

'I did.' Ira rummages her chopsticks through the remains of her dinner. They are silent, even dazed. Ira would like to continue her sentence, would like to say: 'And I was puzzled. I felt responsible and then I felt arrogant for feeling responsible. And the whole while, I just felt like I wasn't feeling enough, or feeling the wrong things.'

She watches as the bloated skin of a dumpling floats to the surface of the tepid soup.

'Ira,' Kit says, 'I missed you today.'

The waiter comes to clear their dishes and Ira settles the bill. On the walk home, without explicitly agreeing to it, they take a different route from the night before. They pass a billboard that, at this moment, displays an advertisement for Icebreakers, but Ira suspects Kit has already developed other interests, as if each product in his care were a satellite shot into space that eventually eases into its own self-sustaining orbit.

They have one more exchange about Mr Carroll before they go to sleep, and Ira wonders if it will be the last they speak of him.

'I hope at one time he was happy.'

'I hope so too.'

Overnight, the public transport authorities clean the last of Mr Carroll's blue writing from the walls. In Saturday's news update there might be murmurings about taxpayer dollars. To the next day's commuters it will appear that reality has reset itself; even the train tracks will gleam with new polish, but to Ira it will be more like a palimpsest that can never be satisfactorily wiped clean. Kit holds her more tenderly than he normally would, and in the morning they wake up to roses.

EIGHTEEN BELLS KARAOKE CASTLE (SING YOUR HEART OUT)

3! 2! 1! If you want a guaranteed night of FUN at a FULLY LICENSED VENUE that is VALUE FOR MONEY and CLOSE TO PUBLIC TRANSPORT, then you'll love Eighteen Bells Karaoke Castle, Perth's premiere karaoke destination. In the heart of the city with a view of the Old Swan River, boasting a catalogue of over 800,000 songs and a mouth-watering menu of authentic Asian cuisine, Eighteen Bells Karaoke Castle will give you and your friends an unforgettable interactive musical rollercoaster ride For! Your! Heart!

Did you know? The word *karaoke* is derived from the Japanese *kara* meaning 'empty' and *ōketsutora* meaning 'orchestra'. An establishment where people gather to engage in karaoke is known as a *karaoke box*. Eighteen Bells Karaoke Castle is located on the former site of the Ritz–Carlton hotel, adjacent to the heritage-listed Bell Tower. It is more than a box! At Eighteen Bells, we offer a completely nostalgic karaoke encounter. You'll swear it's the year 2000 again.

Oh! I am Pikelet. I do not actually know what this place was like in the year 2000. As you can see I was born in the Year of the Rabbit. Did you know? There are over one hundred rooms in Eighteen Bells Karaoke Castle, including ten large function rooms that can be hired for twenty-first birthday parties, weddings, and funerals. You might be surprised to learn that we are a popular venue for funerals! I think songs are important to the living and the dead. When I die I would like my relatives to sing 'Turn to Stone' by Electric Light Orchestra because it is my favourite song.

Oh, but my family doesn't live here anymore. It was my sister Victoria who got me this job. Initially she recommended that I work the children's parties at Eighteen Bells. I don't think she realised how insensitive this suggestion was. A lot of people born in the Year of the Rabbit end up employed in children's entertainment even if not all of us are actually suited to that line of work and are okay with being touched and cuddled and so forth. I am quite shy and I am not good at being playful. However, I do not mind scrubbing vomit out of carpet and negotiating with inebriated clients, which makes me an ideal night worker at Eighteen Bells, even if my giant lagomorph body is not good at manoeuvring through tight spaces.

I do not mean to make it sound like Eighteen Bells is an unhappy place. I think it is more accurate to say that most people are simply unhappy—here and everywhere—and don't actually realise it.

Did you know? Even though the *Karaoke Fun Times Licensing Act 2019* means that karaoke boxes can show original music videos without infringing copyright, most clients at Eighteen Bells prefer to view generic footage. This is what makes Eighteen Bells so popular: clients can choose whether to sing along to the original music video or to generic footage that simulates the stock footage which was common in karaoke boxes at the turn of the millennium. So you can sing 'Ironic' to moving images of Alanis Morissette wailing and pounding her head against a car seat, or you can sing 'Ironic' to 'Happy Cute Caucasian Man Smiling In Forrest Chase' or 'Beautiful Young Multiethnic Couple Taking Self-Portrait Photo In AQWA'.

It is these local videos that are most popular, especially if they depict beloved Perth locations from before the Year of Unprecedented Ecological Terror. The most popular video is 'Attractive Caucasian Woman Laughing In Kings Park'. I like this video too. The lady in the video is running barefoot through Kings Park in slow motion and she keeps turning to look over her shoulder and smile at the camera—smile at *you*. Every time she turns, her long brown hair fans out, and you can see that her teeth are very white, and in the background you can make out skyscrapers and the Narrows Bridge and peaceful morning traffic. I find that this video is best accompanied by 'Call Me Maybe' by Carly Rae Jepsen.

Anyway, the reason why I think most people are unhappy without realising it is that people cry a lot at karaoke, and not just drunk people. I was working a big thirtieth birthday party last week and when I crept into the room to ask if the clients wanted to extend their session for another hour there were two women holding each other singing 'Wrecking Ball' by Miley Cyrus while thick long tracks of tears slid through their make-up. I looked around the room and all the other partygoers were silently watching '2017 Sculpture By The Sea, Cottesloe Beach', which isn't even one of our Top 100 videos—because there aren't people in it and it's not even a proper video, more like a montage—but what was that look on their faces? Hurt, longing. Something in that lost blue ocean cut deep and quick like glass, and they could not stop their sadness from billowing out.

People often assume that those of us born in the Year of the Rabbit are simple-minded, but I think I can be smart sometimes. Did you know? Eighteen Bells is so named because of the eighteen Swan Bells, which are housed in the nearby heritage-listed Bell Tower which was built to commemorate the turn of the millennium. You can see the Bell Tower in its former glory in 'Lonely Attractive Woman Walks Around Barrack Street Jetty, Checks Smart Phone For Text Messages, Trails Hand Through Water In Decorative Fountain'.

Victoria remembers what the Bell Tower was like. She

is actually quite a lot older than me but I forget sometimes because of how quickly I outgrew her. She says the Bell Tower wasn't all that remarkable on the outside, really—all spire and no tower, she likes to say—but when you were on the inside you could see the bells arrayed like giant seeds inside a pod, and for a gold coin you could make the bells somersault on their wheels, throwing their bulk forward, and for all their terrifying weight the sounds they produced were light and clear as the first thoughts of the morning.

Like I said, my family doesn't live here anymore. They moved to New Zealand following the Year of Seven Different Prime Ministers. My mother said that this country is cursed, falling apart (literally—the Sydney Opera House had just collapsed for the third time when my parents made the decision to move). I was meant to go with them, but what fate awaited me in a new home? New Zealand had the lowest rate of Year of the Rabbit births; most of the children died before the age of five or got relocated to Australia. How could I expect to find acceptance there? Here, I have my work at Eighteen Bells. Here, I have 800,000 songs and endless videos of how this city used to be.

You can probably tell that I miss Victoria. I have no doubt that my parents love me, but Victoria was my first friend, and my first official best friend. It's true! When Victoria was eleven and I was three we carved 'VICKY &&&& PIKE BEST FRIENDS FOR LIFE' into the coffee table. The extra ampersands were there because we had just learned how to draw ampersands and we each wanted a turn to carve one, and then another one. Mum and Dad were furious for days.

Victoria was the one who introduced me to karaoke. She had her eighteenth birthday party at Eighteen Bells. I wasn't going to go originally, but Victoria said that some of her friends also had Year of the Rabbit siblings or cousins and nobody would make fun of me. I went along and tried to make myself small in the corner, which is hard when you're a giant rabbit. Victoria's birthday is in spring, too, so I was moulting everywhere. Nobody made fun of me, but nobody tried to include me either. Finally, at the end of the second hour, vibrating with her first-ever legal cocktail (I think it was the Sasha Fierce Triple Threat—Kahlúa, Krupnik, and Sassolino), Victoria forcibly enlisted me in a duet of 'Rock Lobster' by The B-52s. She made me do the non-lyrical bits like *scoo-doo-bi-dup!* and *ooh-wah!* I think she was trying to be kind by giving me the vocal part with no lyrics, but then it got to the call-and-response bit of the song where the male vocalist namechecks various animals like the stingray and the manta ray and several others that probably don't exist anymore, and a female vocalist makes a different animal sound for each animal. But, the thing is, standing there in front of all of my sister's friends, I couldn't remember what sounds were in the original song, so, instead, I produced an unvarying piercing scream for every single animal. Then I ran away to the bathroom and hid there, moulting, until Mum came to pick us up.

But a strange thing happened. Victoria's friends wanted me to come with them to karaoke again. 'Where is your screaming bunny sister?' they would say. And they weren't being mean; they actually wanted me around. It's only now, after three years of working at Eighteen Bells, that I understand. It doesn't matter what you do at karaoke. It doesn't matter if you can't sing. As long as you sing with conviction.

Does that sound trite? Sorry! I'm being serious though. I think people become their truest selves at Eighteen Bells. Or, perhaps, they *remember* their truest selves, the self that was there the whole time. Even if skyscrapers and shopping centres keep falling down and the ocean is pink and congeals in the wintertime, the city is still the city, you know?

I am turning eighteen in March. I know I am one of the lucky ones. I wonder if other Year of the Rabbit children will have their eighteenth birthday parties at Eighteen Bells. I wonder how many of us are left. Did you know? It is impossible for scientists to determine the average lifespan of a Year of the Rabbit child. In fact, I think it is impossible for anyone to say anything certain about us as long as there are a few still alive.

Huh? Why would my family move away if I could die at any minute? Well, they want me to be happy and safe, and I want them to be happy and safe. And I mean that as hard as I meant every single one of my 'Rock Lobster' screams. And who knows! Maybe I won't die a Year of the Rabbit–related death. Maybe I'll die in an accident. Maybe I'll catch my ear in a revolving door, or I'll be watching a movie and the cinema complex will collapse, or I'll be standing tippy-toe at the supermarket to reach for a box of cereal and the shelf will fall over and crush me.

I feel that I am doing something important here. I know it doesn't seem like much: serving beer and Sasha Fierce Triple Threats to clients, teaching them how to use the touchscreen, politely telling them not to jump on the furniture, cleaning up their glasses and stained napkins after they're gone, spritzing the room with air freshener for the next clients. When the clients' final hour is up they always say, 'Just one more song!' Like they're dreaming and they don't want to wake up just yet, locked in communion with a self they only half-remember, filling the empty orchestra with everything inside their heart. And I know what that feels like. Just one more song, just one more hour, just one more day.

Huh? You want to get a video of me singing? Okay. How about … no! No, I don't wanna do 'Rock Lobster'! Ha ha ha ha ha! Hey? Electric Light Orchestra? Yeah, yeah let's do that!

Will you sing too? It's okay if it makes you sad.

Okay.

Which video? How about 'Group Of Multiethnic Young People Dancing At Sundowner Party On Ritz-Carlton Hotel Rooftop'?

Okay!

Ha ha ha ha ha!

Don't worry! You'll know when to start because there'll be a countdown, see?

3!

2!

1!

SMART OVENS FOR
LONELY PEOPLE

After that day at the overpass I was assigned an oven. It was manufactured by a company known for its cutting-edge cuteness. This oven was called Neko Oven because it was shaped like a giant cat's head. It had a rounded chamber, a triangular-eared hood, and an alarm that sounded very much like the jingle of a cat's bell.

The oven was covered by my insurance. Let me be clear, though: my Neko Oven was not at all like those gauche models featured in the commercials, the ones in which sexily deep-voiced ovens whisper/bake sweet nothings for sad single people. Neko Oven was quite classy actually. She (for Neko Oven was programmed with a female voice) was fond of kindly but firmly stating the limits of her responsibilities. *That is not my function*, she'd say when I would ask her if she thought I was ready to unblock Adam from my newsfeed, or whether she could recommend any forms of self-harm that were relatively harmless, like holding ice cubes. That is not my function, she would say sedately, and then, Would you like some shepherd's pie?

No, nobody could accuse Neko Oven of being an enabler. Because she couldn't do everything by herself. For the first week she just sat in my kitchen in her cat-shaped cardboard carton. There's no way to guarantee that a person assigned their oven will actually even get around to activating it. Perhaps there's some smug clinical reasoning for that, like: in order for recovery to work, the client must independently arrive at a place where they are ready to accept help. To peel back that first strip of packing tape from the box.

That was the day of Lydia's disastrous kitchen tea. It turns out that your love for a dear friend does not negate the crushing tedium of having to study the minutiae of her courtship with her future husband. Because Lydia had decided that in order to control the queue for the buffet she would require guests to first complete some kind of diabolical Sudoku–crossword hybrid puzzle about her and her fiancé. 1, Across: Where did Lydia and Liam meet? 2, Down: What did Lydia and Liam eat on their first date? 3, Across: What is the date of Lydia and Liam's dating anniversary? 4, Down: What is the date of Lydia and Liam's engagement anniversary?

On and on and on. That was the day I learnt, via Lydia's aunt, how to say 'This is bullshit' in French (*C'est des conneries*).

Perhaps it was this lingering kinship with the puckered aunt's *crise de colère* that compelled me to finally set up Neko Oven.

And that was it—the hard part, over. Neko Oven awoke with three crisp bell notes, synced herself with the fridge and pantry, and asked me to grate two carrots, please. The first meal she made for me was a frittata. A frittata is typically one of the first meals a smart oven makes for you because it's easy to hide vegetables and stale ingredients in the egg mixture. It was a golden, hopeful start to our relationship: Neko Oven was going to take my meagre, wilted scraps and turn them into something silky and nutritious.

Just like her feline namesake, Neko Oven was self-cleaning. I sat at the kitchen table reading her instruction manual and the terms of her hire period as she rumbled softly through her wash cycle. I was covered for one year with Neko Oven, with the potential for an extension of another six months pending a progress report from Neko Oven herself.

Would you like me to play some light music? Neko Oven asked, once she was done sloshing herself with sudsy water. She played a little sample of 'God Only Knows' by The Beach Boys, but, due to licensing issues, she rendered it entirely with her little range of bell sounds.

'I'm sorry I took so long to unpack you,' I said.

It's okay, she said. And then:

You don't have to be sorry anymore.

I ended up discarding most of the frittata leftovers. Neko Oven didn't say a word about it, and would never say a word about anything I wasted, and I learned, just like she said on that first night, not to be sorry all the time.

Adam heard about what happened and arranged to meet me for coffee. He came straight from rehearsal and he was still wearing his character's clothes, a dress shirt and pressed suit pants and suspenders. I had arrived unwisely early and was already seated when he showed—perhaps it was up to me to rise and hug him in greeting, but I didn't. He stacked his phone and keys on the table and I caught sight, then, of an unfamiliar ornament on his keychain: a mini silver Eiffel Tower. My mind itched with speculations.

'How are you?' he asked in that hushed, cautious voice everyone was using around me.

'Okay,' I said. 'How are you?'

And, relieved, he told me about his new production, repeating facts that he'd forgotten he'd already told me, and he kept saying, 'I feel like I'm really pushing myself as an actor.' He sat close to the edge of his seat as if he was only going to stay for a minute, and he kept reviving his phone to check the time, and I kept pretending not to notice. He smelled of muscular body spray and car upholstery.

And once the warm-up talk was over it was time for him to say: 'So. You almost died.'

'Yeah.'

I felt once again the rush of morning traffic, the arms of

a stranger.

And what was that look, in Adam's eyes? Actual sadness? Or a kind of perfunctory empathy, the detection of a blip in his beautiful universe, something to rectify as soon as possible so he could keep sailing on?

He asked if I was still getting therapy. If I was still living alone. If Lydia was looking after me, if my mother was looking after me, if Biljana and the others at work knew about what happened. Perhaps he wanted to reassure himself that he didn't have to do more than this one coffee meeting, a quick hour between appointments.

'I'm glad you're doing better now, Shu,' he said.

He checked his phone again and this time I noticed that the background of his lock screen was a selfie of him with his arm around a woman I'd never seen before. Coldness crept over me.

There wasn't much more to say after that. Adam said he had to go, and when he crossed the street to his car his eyes were already on his phone, swiping a text message. He drove off without looking back.

⬤

On the way home I bought frozen peas, mini Roma tomatoes, beef mince close to expiry. I bought Dutch cream potatoes, dried pasta shells, chicken stock cubes, jasmine rice.

Please peel seven potatoes, Neko Oven said.

Please dice the potatoes into cubes.

Please place the potatoes in a saucepan of salty water.

Please place the saucepan on my left burner.

I was doing what psychologists call *ruminating*. I was *indulging in unhelpful thinking*. I was listening to a mixtape I'd made for Adam back when we were dating. The theme of the mixtape was hugging and included songs like 'Throw Your Arms Around Me' by Hunters & Collectors. I wasted all of the best hugging songs on a relationship that lasted less than a year.

Do you know the difference between a shepherd's pie and a cottage pie?

'No.'

A shepherd's pie is traditionally made with minced lamb or mutton, whereas a cottage pie is traditionally made with minced beef. So actually we are making a cottage pie.

They looked to be near the Swan River, at a wedding, perhaps—Adam was wearing a tie and there were white chairs in the background of the lock screen photo. Their eyes were small from the sunlight; they were smiling. How did they meet? How long had they been together? Who was getting married—a cousin of Adam's, perhaps? He never invited me to family events when we were dating. He never changed his lock screen to a photo of us.

Please dice one onion finely.

Please cut the mini Roma tomatoes into quarters.

There was a pile of laundry that needed washing; there

were stiff clothes hanging on the collapsible washing line I'd set up in the living room a week ago. I hadn't changed my bedsheets for nearly three months, which meant they were the same sheets I'd slept in on that day at the overpass. Everywhere there seemed to be indictments of my failure to meet some low bar of adulthood—fallen hair coiled in drain holes, unopened bills, white dried spots of toothpaste on the bathroom counter.

Please season the mince with salt and pepper.

Please fry the onions in a little bit of olive oil.

Was she working on the same production as him? Was she an actress, a lighting technician, a stage manager? How soon after breaking up with me did he meet her? Is she funnier than me? Is she better at sex than me? Did she know he met me for coffee that day? Did she pity me?

'Those same damn bottles going out and those same damn bottles coming back.'

Pardon?

I froze. I wondered what would happen if I didn't respond to Neko Oven—whether she would just ask the same question again and again.

'Sorry. That's just something I say sometimes. When I'm having repetitive thoughts. Because I feel like I'm a survivor on a deserted island, throwing messages in glass bottles into the sea, only for the tide to keep bringing them back. *Those same damn bottles going out and those same damn bottles coming back.*'

I wondered if Neko Oven had any notion of survivors on deserted islands. If a machine understood loneliness, or repetitive thoughts, or talking to oneself.

I see.

And then, hopefully:

So you say this phrase in the manner of a mantra?

I smiled. 'Kind of like a mantra, yeah.'

After Neko Oven had been activated for two weeks she sent a recommendation to Biljana to let me return to work. Biljana gave me a hug when I arrived at the shop, a rare gesture, and it was strange to discover that underneath those billowy kaftans was a small sculpted body. She let me focus on alterations all day and jumped up to attend to customers before I could even lift my eyes from my machine.

On my lunchbreak I used the kitchenette microwave to heat up a little plastic container of Neko Oven's leftovers (some kind of casserole she'd improvised from tinned chickpeas, bacon, and gin) and took it to the food court to eat alone. It was nearly two o'clock, so the food court was empty except for cappuccino-sipping seniors and other workers on their lunchbreaks, their uniform hats or aprons scrunched up in their laps, scrolling through their newsfeeds, squeezing black drops of soy sauce onto their sushi from little fish-shaped tubes.

I was doing that mindfulness thing that my psychologist told me to do—where I would notice five things I could see, five things I could hear, five things I could feel—when I heard someone say: 'Shu?'

And there was Lydia, holding a lacquered wooden ampersand and two lacquered wooden *L*s that she'd just purchased from Typo.

I stood up, and she put her wooden letters down on the table and flung her arms around me. She said she was sorry we didn't get the chance to talk properly at the kitchen tea, and that she'd still love for me to be a bridesmaid, but after what happened she didn't want to make demands on me, but also she didn't want me to think that she thought that I couldn't handle the commitment of being a bridesmaid. Also, Liam had already asked three of his friends to be groomsmen and she really wanted the sides to be even so if I couldn't be a bridesmaid she'll have to ask somebody else because it'd be awkward to demote a groomsman after they've all already said yes and put down deposits on matching suits.

'No, of course, I understand,' I said. 'And I'm happy to be your bridesmaid. For sure.' I was about to apologise for stressing her out, but then I remembered that Neko Oven said I didn't need to be sorry anymore.

'Good. Oh, good. I'm so glad.' And then Lydia's eyes softened. I braced myself. 'And how *are* you?' she asked. 'Back at work today?'

I told her that I was in the smart oven program. I pointed

at my lunch with pride. Lydia clapped appreciatively. She asked me what model I had, so I told her about Neko Oven. I described her cat-shaped hood and her bell sounds and her sedate non-judgemental voice.

'Oh, Shu!' Lydia exclaimed. 'That's just wonderful.'

And then she said: 'You know, it's like I've always said: living all by yourself, all alone in that apartment—you really need a cat. A really cute cat. So you won't be lonely. So you'll have some company.' Lydia smiled. 'And now you have one.'

'It's just patronising, that's all,' I said to Neko Oven later while I was separating the squashed mini Roma tomatoes from the firmer ones. 'She always used to suggest I get a pet cat. Whenever she'd ask how I was going and I'd say that I was lonely or I missed Adam or I hadn't talked to anybody besides customers for three days straight.'

Neko Oven blinked her lights speculatively, but didn't say anything. She adjusted the heat on one of her burners.

'I mean—she doesn't *mean* it to be patronising. She doesn't know that she's saying something that I get all the time. Especially from people who are in relationships already. That's the thing. It only ever comes from people who are happily coupled off. *Why don't you get a cat, Shu?* Then they go off on their date nights and upload gorgeous photos to Instagram.'

Please slice the mini Roma tomatoes into halves, Neko

Oven said, so I did.

'Should I tell Lydia not to say things like that? What do you think I should do?'

. That is not my function.

Of course.

I concentrated on the sound of the knife hitting the bottom of the chopping board. The acidic fragrance of over-ripe tomatoes.

But it is true what you say, Neko Oven conceded. There are limitations to the care that a pet or a smart oven can provide to a human.

She started to ping out a song with her bell tones. At first I thought she was ad-libbing, but then I figured out that the tune was 'Wuthering Heights' by Kate Bush, which had absolutely no relevance to the discussion at hand. She was always doing things like that. I kept thinking about Lydia. I wanted absurdly to make her feel bad for making me feel bad.

Those same damn bottles going out, Neko Oven said.

Those same damn bottles coming back.

I'd had Neko Oven for about three months when I saw the stranger again. We were waiting on opposite platforms at the train station, the only two people there. There was no uncertainty, no double-takes—we knew immediately. He was even wearing the same grey-and-green striped hoodie which had caught my eye that fateful morning. For a moment we just looked at each other from across the tracks; he lifted his hand in a sheepish wave. Then he picked up his shopping bags, climbed the stairs, and crossed over to my platform. 'It's good to see you again,' he said.

'It's good to see you too,' I said, which was the truth, even though I was embarrassed.

'I never said thank you,' he said, 'for what you did that day.'

'I never said thank you either,' I said.

He smiled a little. 'What are the odds? Two people choosing the same overpass to jump from. The same time, the same day.'

'Yeah.'

We stood next to each other for a long time. An abandoned babycino, cup was rocking back and forth on the train tracks, a thin smile of chocolate stuck to the bottom.

'Would you say that you're okay now?' I asked the stranger.

'Would you?'

'No.'

'No.'

'The next train to—Perth—departs in—five minutes,' came the announcement, but, with the stranger next to me, I couldn't help but hear the announcement in Neko Oven's melodious and measured voice. I wondered if we should even be talking to each other.

'Still,' the stranger said, 'I guess we keep going.'

His voice creaked like the broken spine of a Bible. One of his fraying green shopping bags contained baked beans, bananas, dried spaghetti, tinned tuna, and as he rearranged his grip on the handles I noticed he was wearing a wedding ring. The sight of it zapped me, a truth I'd always known: having someone who loves you doesn't exempt you from wanting to die.

'The worst thing,' he said, as if he heard my last thought, 'is not being able to explain why.'

Why.

Why.

When people asked, 'How *are* you?' did they really mean, '*Why* did you?'

His train was about to arrive, so we said goodbye. He climbed the stairs, lifting his legs in a broken gait that I recognised in myself, the green shopping bags sagging, as if they, too, were ready for things to end.

♦

Because I was tired.

Because I wanted to die, the same way you might want a drink of water, or want to sleep, or want someone to love you back.

Because staying alive took so much work. All that searching oneself for the problem, fumbling for a way to articulate the problem; all that getting out of bed, sliding into cold clothes, spooning cereal from bowl to mouth.

And the appointments. A doctor and a trail of invoices for every failing part of me—eyes, skin, brain, teeth, waistline, uterus, heart.

Because I realised that it was my biological imperative to die, that dying was my body's default function. My whole body, conspiring to die, dedicated to the task of dying.

Because I was bored. Because it was boring to sleep. Because it was boring to retell the story to each new therapist, crisis hotline operator, psychiatrist. Because listening to the same guided meditation tracks was boring. Because the compulsive dragged thumb, hold, release, refresh on an inert newsfeed was boring. Because crying was boring. Because being unable to cry was boring. Because the white walls and bedsheets and the hollowed indent in the mattress were boring.

Because I couldn't call anybody, even though that's what people say—*you can call me anytime.* To say what? I am bored? I am sad? I want to die?

Because I'd tried therapy. I'd tried escitalopram, duloxetine, desvenlafaxine. I'd tried phoning a friend. I'd tried Pilates and focusing on the breath. I'd tried being curious about my feelings. I'd tried thinking of five things I was grateful for. I'd tried thinking: the sky is blue, the grass is green.

But I hadn't tried dying.

I told Neko Oven about meeting the stranger from the overpass as I was slicing an eggplant. We were making Moussaka. She didn't interrupt me at all, just blinked her lights occasionally to let me know that she was listening.

How do you feel about the encounter? she asked when I was finished.

'I don't know. I don't know if it did any good.'

Conversations do not need to do good or bad. They can just be conversations.

'That's true.'

If we were to apply your metaphor about messages inside bottles, we could say that you discovered new bottles on the shore of your solitary island, a fresh reminder that there are other islands and other people throwing bottles, that while you are alone on your island you are not alone in the ocean.

'I guess so.'

Such a reminder is neither good nor bad. It is just information.

A neutral fact.

The ocean is full of bottles.

That is why I and others like me exist.

It is time to fry the eggplant.

I placed the frying pan on her left burner. I drizzled olive oil into the pan. 'How long on average do people need their smart oven?' I asked.

It is difficult to answer your question accurately, said Neko Oven.

Some clients must return their smart oven before they have made a full recovery.

Some clients only use their smart oven for two to four weeks.

Some clients are stable for many months but then undergo a relapse in the final week of their hire period.

Some clients leave the smart oven program and then return intermittently.

She paused. Was Neko Oven really thinking, whenever she paused like that? Wouldn't a machine as smart as her take less than one second to formulate a response to me? Was the pause for my benefit?

She continued:

You could say that the problem is:

(1) the impossibility of quantifying need; and

(2) the non-linearity of recovery.

The day that Lydia and Liam got married was as picturesque and luscious as foretold by Lydia's Pinterest board. The ribbons on the bridesmaids' bouquets matched the colours of the groomsmen's bowties, and as I stood watching my friend glide down the aisle towards a life we'd been taught to want and probably did genuinely want I found that I could be both desperately lonely and profoundly happy; I could always be both.

After the ceremony, I clasped a basket of mini-quiches that Neko Oven helped me to prepare so that the bridal party would have something to eat during the photo shoot. The groomsmen and the other bridesmaids were particularly enthused about the way the crust didn't crumble and scatter pastry everywhere, and I couldn't wait to pass on the compliment to Neko Oven.

Lydia really got her money's worth out of those giant wooden letters: the *L & L* appeared in almost every photo— gathered in Lydia and Liam's arms as they kissed, tangled in Lydia's veil in an overhead shot of Lydia and Liam lying on the lawn, propped on the ground as the bride and her bridesmaids leapt and tossed their bouquets in the air.

Between shooting locations, when nearly all the mini-quiches were gone, Lydia caught my hand and asked how I was going. 'Maybe this is silly of me but I'll be relieved when this is all over,' Lydia said. 'All this—this shouldn't be life.'

'I suppose not,' I said.

This close, she appeared so much like my old friend, only rendered with more vibrant brushstrokes. 'Listen, Shu,' Lydia said, clasping my hand again. The wedding ring gave her hand a new weight. 'I love you so much. I'm so glad you're here.'

I could tell she meant that last part in every single way that the sentence could be meant. She summoned the photographer to take a picture of just us together, and then she went off to join Liam.

I took one of the last mini-quiches from the basket. It fit

so neatly in my hand, this golden vessel; I spied a sundried tomato buried like a jewel close to the surface of the pillow-soft filling. What is the difference between a quiche and a frittata? I made a mental note to ask Neko Oven as I took a bite. It really was true, what everyone was saying: Neko Oven did a fantastic job with the crust.

MOUNTING SEXUAL TENSION BETWEEN TWO LONG-TIME FRIENDS; TOM KNOWS THAT ANT IS A SPY BUT ANT DOESN'T

'I wish you would just tell me.'

Ant gazes across the kitchen at Tom, who is still sweaty from his morning run—tight jaw glistening, unworn earbuds hanging over the darkened neckline of his T-shirt. Tom tips water into his mouth from a crushed Mount Franklin bottle, and Ant watches Tom's nervous swig slide down Tom's throat. A hard lump of tension, tangible as an egg.

'There's nothing to tell you, Ant.'

'I won't be mad. I promise. I wasn't mad that time you ditched my phone into a storm drain.'

Tom snorts, like *can you believe this guy*, but Ant continues:

'It wasn't an accident. I know because you received a text on your phone and then you snatched my phone out of my hand and threw it down the storm drain. That's a difficult thing to do not-on-purpose.'

'You're still mad about that?'

'No, I'm not mad. This has been well-established. And now you're trying to derail the conversation, but this conversation is about me asking you to tell me the truth about the matching Glock pistols in our respective underwear drawers and the identical emergency briefcases of cash in nine different currencies sequestered behind secret panels in our wardrobes.'

'How did you even get in here, Ant?'

'*Again*, you are trying to derail the conversation, but the answer to your question is that I know how to pick locks. Did you know that I know how to pick locks? I certainly didn't know that I knew how to pick locks, just like I didn't know that we had matching Glocks and briefcases, which is the topic of this conversation.'

'I replaced your phone with an even better one and your new phone number ends in "268" which spells "ANT", which you admitted was convenient.'

'Are you in the same conversation that I am in, Tom? I wish you would join me in this conversation that I am having about the Glocks and the briefcases and your unwillingness to be forthcoming.'

Tom drops his Mount Franklin bottle in the kitchen bin. 'Ant, I can't do this right now. I need a shower.'

'And I need some fucking perspicuity, Tom.'

Now Ant slides off the bar stool. He walks towards Tom until they are almost chest-to-chest—close enough to smell Tom, damp and tight and pissed off. There is a soft tinny song spurting out of Tom's hanging earbuds.

Tom swallows. Ant leans in.

'Stop trying to protect me, Tom. It's getting old.'

Tom groans. He takes a step back, but it's too late; the moment has twisted like a screw. Ant's expression hasn't changed. Tom bravely affects a laugh.

'Well, Ant. I suppose this is the part of the conversation where you recall some telling moment from our adolescence where I protected you to the detriment of both of us. Which one will you choose? The one about how I beat up Tristan Lombard at the sports carnival when he called you a chink?'

'Oh, not at all. That was far too satisfying. You decommissioned his pelvis. No, I was going to go for the time you tried to obscure the fact that Jessica Aubrey turned me down for the river cruise in favour of *Richard Kronemeyer*, that clod with the light-up shoes. There are only so many times you can suddenly yank my attention to some other point-of-focus, *while we are on the river cruise*, while Kronemeyer is lighting up the dance floor with his fucking light-up shoes.'

'From our rich and complicated history, you would pick that incident?'

'We *do* have a rich and complicated history, don't we, Tom? Rich, chocolatey, complicated history, with notes of deceit. Tell me about the Glocks.'

Ant paces the perimeter of the kitchen. Tom scratches his stubble.

'I need a shower, Ant.'

'Strange choice, Glocks. Kind of dull. Generic. Discount-bin firearm.'

'Ant.'

'Can't get too attached to it. You wouldn't miss it if you dropped it in, say, a storm drain. The *briefcases*, on the other hand—very handsome. The glossiest and most threatening of leathers. Confident handgrip. Snappy buckles. Smooth, impenetrable, Don't-Fuck-With-Me briefcases. The combination is the date that we graduated from university.'

Ant comes to rest in front of Tom again.

'Charming personal touch, Tom.'

'Ant.'

Tom rests the five fingers of his left hand on Ant's chest, briefly.

'Shower. I need one. I can't have this conversation now.'

'Sure you can,' Ant says. 'Have a filthy conversation while you're covered in filth.'

Tom says nothing. There's a different look in his eyes now. Soft and sad and hurt. A little crumple of the lids. Fuck.

Tom shifts closer. He folds his hands around Ant's shoulders.

'Please.'

A password can be a pilchard or a peephole or a pomegranate seed.

It can have several teeth.

Who invented the password?

The story goes that the Romans invented perimeter defence and the password.

In the insufficient light of the moon, while the military encampment slept in circle upon circle of tents, an approaching friend would be indistinguishable from an approaching foe.

The task of the sentry was to challenge anyone sighted. The call was, 'Halt!' and then, 'Who goes there?'

To utter the password was to authenticate oneself and issue a command: Let me in.

A password can be a brooch or a perfume or an upturned letter on a public sign.

A password complements the shape of the lock.

'Tom!'

Ant beats on the bathroom door.

'*Tom*. There are two alternative points of egress in your bathroom and three if you oil up enough to squeeze through the vent, and before you came home I sabotaged all three of them.'

'[Unintelligible].'

'What?'

The faucet squeaks off. The drain gurgles. Ant presses his ear against the bathroom door.

'Tom. You have been showering for seven minutes now. Quit stalling. *Tom.*'

The door drops suddenly and Ant nearly topples into Tom. Tom, towel-wrapped from the waist-down, hair darkened and wet and bristling, face soured by the least relaxing shower ever. That tic in his jaw starts up again.

'Excuse me.'

Tom doesn't wait for Ant to move, but brushes past him, leaving a streak of moistness on Ant's bare arm. Ant watches Tom's glistening shoulder blades disappear into the master bedroom. He trails after him.

'Tell me about the Glocks. The Glocks. The Glocks. The Glocks.'

'Do you think you could leave me alone for a few minutes so I can change?'

'The Glocks. The Glocks. The Glocks. The Glocks.'

'Get the *fuck* out, Ant!'

It's a too-sudden tonal shift, as if Tom is attempting, belatedly, to be angry. He even shoves Ant, just a flat ineffectual one-handed shove while his other hand grips the knot of towel around his waist. Tom wavers for a moment, and then decides to commit to this new tack completely. He snarls:

'For *fuck*'s sake. You think I could ever lie to you? Do you think I would ever do something to fuck you over? After all these years? I have *always* been there for you. *Always*. From the very first. Fuck you, Ant.'

And yet Ant doesn't move away. He matches Tom's glare. 'Listen, you dick. You broke into my home and planted a Glock and a briefcase in some very private places and *I know it was you*. Now: are you done with your feeble little fugue of denial? Because let me tell you. You are *not* pulling it off.'

And Tom grabs Ant. They smash together on the carpet. The shock of the fall rings in their ears; the room seesaws and settles. Tom's chest heaves—he is tremoring, all shower-softened and sweet smelling—but Ant is completely still. Tom can see himself reflected in Ant's two dark moons.

Ant gazes up at Tom. His breath is warm.

Ant whispers:

'What are you so scared of?'

It is difficult to say who kisses whom first. Perhaps, in the way of best friends, the movement is synchronous, prefigured telepathically. Tom leans in and Ant cranes his neck and their mouths grapple in wet hot collision. Tom holds Ant's cheeks as if Ant's face is a bowl from which he wants to drink and drink water, so precious is each sip, and Ant clasps Tom's slick warm biceps and kisses Tom in short desperate bursts. Tom whines, scrabbles on top of Ant, bumps into Ant's hard-on. The button of Ant's shorts has already slithered loose, the zipper yielding, and Tom wriggles his hand past the waistband of Ant's boxers. Ant bucks a little. Tom's conscious of the towel sliding off his waist, his damp showered limbs, Ant's hands on his ass. The keen tight weight of his own desire. Unpractised, unrehearsed, Ant slips Tom's cock inside the cool grasp of his hand, hooks his thumb around the shaft, and Tom has to moan, has to steady himself with his hand spread on Ant's chest, breath shuddering through bared teeth, while Ant moves his fingers gently, experimentally, like a beginner gripping a violin, testing the strings, sliding up and down the fingerboard. If Ant cared to he could count Tom's ribs, straining so close against Tom's skin; he reaches up his spare hand to trawl his fingers across the ridges like the spines of books. Tom quakes, whines. He clenches Ant's T-shirt.

And when he comes he marvels that such disparate emotions can produce the same thrill.

Shame, love, ecstasy.

Ant strokes Tom's hair.

'It's okay. Don't cry.'

A password can be a pearl or an oyster or a deep sea diver.

The best passwords have complex teeth.

The password of the Roman army was reset daily. The military tribune scribed the new password on wooden tablets, which were circulated throughout the camp and returned to the tribune's tent.

The password was so important that if a tablet were to fail

to make it back to the tribune's tent, the soldier responsible was punished.

To forget the password brought its own punishment.

But could we also agree that a forgettable password is a failed password?

A password can be a griffin or an archer or a fortified tower.

It should not have too many teeth.

A password is a key and a command.

Let me in.

Before long the day turns amber. Ant and Tom are supine for the moment, spread out on Tom's bed, letting the breeze from the open window whisk the sweat from their skin. Tom breaks the silence by leaning over the edge of the bed to pluck another tissue from the crumpled box. Tom wipes a small pool of cum off his stomach, scrunches up the tissue, and drops it on the carpet with the other scrunched-up tissues. The movement inspires Ant to lift his head a little to re-examine his crotch but his hasty mop-up seems to have been sufficient. Ant and Tom aren't really sure if it matters anyway. The etiquette of the situation escapes them.

Before the moment can become too awkward, Tom slides close to Ant and kisses him. Outside a dog barks. Once, twice.

'Are we assassins, Tom?'

Tom curls his head underneath Ant's chin. He kisses Ant's collarbone and traces it with his finger as a novice reader might trace a difficult passage of text.

'Close,' Tom says. 'We are spies.'

'What's the difference?'

'I should think that would be obvious. A matter of intent.'

'How can I be a spy if I don't know what I am spying on? Unless *you* are the spy, and *I* am the assassin.'

'I suppose that, if we are to be precise, you are the spy and I am your handler.'

'My *handler*. What a romantic and utilitarian term.'

'Shh.'

Tom lifts himself up on one elbow to kiss Ant again. They form a wet humid cave with their mouths.

'I'm serious, Tom. How can I be a spy? I haven't been spying on anyone. What is my directive?'

'I don't know what your directive is.'

'But you're my handler.'

Tom sighs tenderly. He traces Ant's collarbone again and decides it's one of his favourite corners of Ant's body.

Tom says, 'Our mission is so sensitive that I don't know the details. You are the only one out of you and me who has been briefed on the particulars.'

'But I haven't.'

'You have. You just don't remember it.'

Ant's fingers find Tom's fingers. They intertwine.

Ant says, 'I'm "the only one out of you and me who has

been briefed on the particulars"?'

'Yes.'

'That means there are others?'

'Other what?'

'Other spies who have been briefed on the particulars?'

'Please stop using the expression "briefed on the particulars". It sounds ridiculous.'

'You used it first.'

'I'm sorry.'

Their tongues meet again. Tom untangles his hand from Ant's so he can cup Ant's cheek.

'You're right, Ant. We are not the only spy-and-handler team assigned to this particular mission.'

'The mission you know nothing about.'

'Correct.'

'The mission I know about but know nothing about knowing.'

'Yes.'

'Then explain to me your role of handler.'

Despite the open window, the room is very warm. It smells like rucked sweaty bedsheets and dried cum and eager breath. Tom nestles his face in Ant's neck.

'Well, Tom?'

'Hmm?'

'Explain your role as handler to me. I am sure it encompasses more than throwing phones into storm drains.'

Tom laughs. He flips himself onto his back, holding Ant's

hand again.

'I was responsible for setting your activation phrase,' Tom says.

'My activation phrase?'

'Your trigger. Your password. Whatever you want to call it. My directives are as follows. One: protect Anton Chu. Two: protect Thomas Lark. Three: utter Anton Chu's activation phrase when the time comes that Anton Chu requires activation. Four: follow Anton Chu's orders after Anton Chu is activated.'

'How will you know when I need to be activated?'

'I'll receive a signal.'

'You'll be given a signal which signals that you need to signal me. How ornate. Do you have an activation phrase too?'

'No. Just you.'

'And then what happens?'

'You'll remember your directive and you will carry out your directive. I'll be at your disposal.'

'And you have no notion whatsoever as to what my directive is.'

'No.'

'My directive could be to kill you.'

'I doubt that. A handsome amount of time and money has been invested in you and me and others like you and me.'

'When did this investment take place? When were we … recruited?'

Tom caresses Ant's knuckles. He lifts one to his mouth.

Tom asks, 'What do you remember of Baker's Horticulture and Botany class in Year Ten?'

'The distinction between horticulture and botany still eludes me. Baker was never precise about it. Imprecision makes me suspicious, as you know.'

'Well, at any rate, we were the best in Baker's class at remembering taxonomy. And the Latin names of things. Binomial nomenclature. Apparently we were extraordinary at it. That's why they chose us.'

'"They"?'

'Various esoteric high school classes across the country are used to find candidates. So "they" must be some government agency or another. Something shadowy and influential.'

'You don't even know? Why did you agree to this?'

'*We* agreed.'

'Why on Earth did we agree to this?'

'We were good at it, I suppose. The various tests and tasks. It doesn't matter anymore, Ant. Everyone likes to be the thing that fits best.'

'And me being the amnesiac with my memories stuck behind a trigger? Was *that* the best fit?'

Tom's fingers probe the gaps between Ant's knuckles. He searches the ceiling. The blood around Tom's heart is suddenly cold. Ant's small dark gaze is upon him, like the shadow of an owl.

Tom says, 'It was decided—'

'By whom?'

'Well, there was a discussion—'

'A discussion? *We* had a discussion? *We* decided?'

'Yes. We did.'

Tom can't look Ant in the eye, and is ashamed that he can't. He knows that there are all these other questions fidgeting beneath Ant's interrogations.

How long have we loved each other?

How long have you known?

Did I used to know?

Ant says, 'I'm not mad at you, Tom.'

'You sound like you're mad at me.'

'I'm not going to keep on reassuring you that I'm not mad. You are not the party in this conversation that needs reassurance.'

Tom finally risks a glance at Ant, but Ant's face is as smooth and patient as a clock. Their intertwined hands have become sticky with perspiration.

'It could have been me, you know,' Tom says. 'We were equally suited to either role. We settled it with a coin toss.'

Ant frowns.

'It's true, Ant. We knew it was an important decision. It would change everything. We wagged Human Bio and sat at the far end of the oval, near the abandoned demountables. It was just turning into spring; the grass was damp. Each of us wanted to spare the other the confusion of being the one in the dark. We used a fifty-cent piece. You called heads. The next time we went on a Botany field trip, you started to attend different training sessions to me. You weren't allowed to tell me what you learnt. I think ...'

Tom leans over and lightly touches Ant's temple.

'I think they made it so that you *couldn't* tell me what you'd learnt.'

Tom spreads his fingers and Ant tips his face into Tom's palm and closes his eyes. His exhaled breath prickles Tom's fingers.

'It's not right, you know,' Ant says. 'We were children.'

'I know, Ant. But we're here now. And I have my directive to protect you.'

Tom draws Ant close. They fold their arms around each other. Tom remembers how tenderly Ant had told him not to cry.

Ant says, 'You said you were the one responsible for setting my activation phrase.'

'Yes. That was the other selection criterion, you see. It wasn't enough to be intelligent. To have exceptional memory recall. They were specifically looking for pairs. Friends. Because of the memory locking procedure.'

'The temporary forgetting procedure.'

'Yes. It's a fussy business.'

'Explain it to me.'

Ant shuffles onto his side. Tom mirrors him so that their eyes are level. That crumple in Tom's eyelid is still there, and Ant allows himself to feel sorry for all the things Tom has carried for the two of them.

Tom says, 'It's your least favourite thing. Imprecise. Trust is always imprecise. It took several sessions. It was almost like hypnosis. Lulling you into something like sleep. I had to write my own script. I had to speak to you in a soft slow voice. I needed you to be completely receptive to me. I needed you to feel safe.'

'And did I?'

Tom reaches out to stroke Ant's feathery fringe. 'You know that I can't speak for you.'

They wriggle closer together until their noses are almost touching.

'Does anybody else know my activation phrase?' Ant asks.

'No, Ant. Just me.'

'What is it?'

'I can't tell you that.'

'Why not?'

'I can't speak it until the proper time.'

'When you receive the signal.'

'Yes.'

'How long have we been waiting?'

'Twelve years, now.'

'And you still remember my activation phrase?'

'Of course. I'll always remember your activation phrase. I thought about it for a very long time.'

A smile flickers on Ant's lips. He catches himself. 'What a strange thing for me to feel delighted about.'

Tom smiles.

'There were very stringent guidelines, you see,' Tom says. 'The activation phrase had to be carefully chosen. I considered and discarded several candidates. I practised them in the mirror. I imagined the day I would say it. I imagined a light snapping on behind your eyes. The memories returning like a rush of blood. I imagined being reunited with some other version of you. Not a better version, or a fuller version, just a different version. I imagined getting to know this other you. All the things we would talk about once our job was done.'

Ant laughs. 'I'm flattered you put so much thought into a limp procession of words.'

And Ant's laugh fades when Tom says:

'But it isn't. Of course it isn't.'

Tom touches Ant's lips. He touches Ant's lashes, his cheekbones, the bridge of his nose, the hollows underneath his eyes.

'I just knew that I wanted it to be beautiful.'

A password can be a seed or a sailcloth or an explosion.

A password is a portal.

I am waiting on the edge of your perimeter. I am stepping into the insufficient light.

I am calling out to you, the watchman. I am laying my sword in the sand. I am opening my arms.

A password can be a whisper between a living person to a just-dead person. The fare paid to the ferryman of the

Underworld. The coins laid on the eyes of a boy who has very far to go.

A password can be a tumour or a melody or a curled finger.

A password complements the shape of the lock.

A password is an intimate organ, a deep secret.

A password is a window to the soul.

Please let me in.

The password is

The bedroom turns to indigo. The same dog barks, once and again. Ant steps through the irregular garden of scrunched-up tissues. He bends down to dip his hand in the pool of clothes on the carpet.

'Are you mad at me, Ant?'

'I told you, I'm not mad. Stop asking.'

'I'm sorry.'

Tom sits on the edge of the bed. He watches Ant pull on his boxers, zip up his shorts, twist into his T-shirt. Tom's towel is still crumpled on the floor, and it will stay that way until the next morning.

Tom asks, 'Will we see each other tomorrow?'

'Of course.'

'You can stay the night, if you want. Please. Will you stay?'

Being naked while Ant is clothed fills Tom with a strange vulnerable desirous feeling. Ant brushes a ball of lint off his T-shirt. It floats across the room like a dandelion seed. Ant sighs, and embraces Tom softly. They kiss in the dying daylight.

'Tomorrow,' says Ant. 'I promise, Tom. I'm not running away. You'll just have to trust me.'

'I'm scared.'

'Scared of what?'

'That you won't come tomorrow.'

'I will come.'

Tom hides his face in Ant's neck. He says:

'I'm scared that the you that comes tomorrow won't be you. That you'll be replaced in the night. That we're both done for now.'

Ant smooths Tom's hair.

'Nobody has to know that I know,' Ant says. 'You haven't disobeyed your directives. Maybe we should have a password too. So you know that the me that stands here stroking your hair is the same me that comes to see you tomorrow. I will knock on your door and say the password and you will know that I am Ant. Your Ant.'

Tom holds Ant's head against his. He feels close to tears without quite knowing why. Ant prompts:

'Something from Baker's class, perhaps. Whatever you like. Whatever you think sounds beautiful. *Passiflora edulis. Actinidia deliciosa. Euphoria longan.*'

Tom moistens his lips. He tastes his inexplicable anxiety. He closes his eyes and tries as hard as he can to feel the warm weight of Ant's hand on the back of his head.

'*Ananas comosus.*'

'*Pyrus pyrifolia.*'

'*Persea americana.*'

'*Solanum lycopersicum.*'

The room is becoming bruised with darkness, and Tom and Ant cradle each other with their heads bent. They whisper softer and softer, like chanting spells.

Mangifera indica. Cucurbita moschata. Punica granatum. Ficus carica.

.PPTX

Everyone has to sit through Brodie's PowerPoint presentation about dinosaurs because it's his birthday and this is everybody's present to him. Pippa gathers with the other housemates in the lounge room, protecting the precarious mound of Cheetos in her cupped hands as she wobbles past the sofa and nestles in the beanbag. The first slide of Brodie's presentation asks the question 'HOW CAN WE POSSIBLY DEFINE WHAT A DINOSAUR IS' and then star-wipes to a bullet list of taxonomic classifications.

Pippa has to bend her head like a bird and eat the Cheetos straight from her palms. It's during one of these little head-dips that she notices Caleb stroking Hannah's hair. Pippa wonders if Hannah knows that Caleb and Lauren made out last night while Hannah was at Pilates. Lauren is playing it very cool, glancing up every now and then from her crochet hook to Brodie's presentation and not looking at Caleb at all.

Pippa feels an absurd flush of jealousy towards all three of them: Caleb, Lauren, Hannah.

'Calling a pterodactyl a dinosaur is a dino-no-no,' says Brodie.

The reason why Pippa knows about Caleb and Lauren is because sometimes Pippa turns invisible. It is as if all the times she is overlooked at parties and at work, all the times she is swiped left on, all the times automatic doors fail to yield to her—it all coalesces into these occurrences of being completely, legitimately unseeable.

So Pippa stood unseen in the kitchen when Caleb touched Lauren's waist, and Lauren tipped her face towards his.

'Please hold your questions until the very end,' says Brodie to Caleb's raised hand.

Pippa is ready to become extinct. She is ready for the roof to collapse, for everybody to survive except for her. She is ready to die unloved, covered in the golden dust of crushed Cheetos. She is ready for her loneliness to enter eternity.

Brodie star-wipes to slide four of 320.

RON SWANSON'S
STENCILLED 'STACHE

1. Autonomous

There. On the main campus of Erdős-Bacon University, on the south side of the Film and Television Studies building, on the concrete wall facing the loading bays and the motorcycle parking: someone had spraypainted a stencilled impression of Ron Swanson from the hit NBC sitcom *Parks and Recreation*. The artist had captured Ron Swanson's croissant-shaped moustache and his aggressive side-part and the twin parentheses of his brows and eye bags: a sturdy face pitted by disdain for skim milk, landscape paintings, and government interference in the private decisions of taxpayers and the free market.

I had retreated here firstly because I had just realised that

George Gershwin's brother Ira had lost power, and secondly because the active competitor, the woman with the typewriter, was playing on my nerves, the way she'd slowly pull a paper out from the rollers and ratchet a new one in. Some of the competitors who had been knocked out in the previous heats had a betting pool going, and I knew that this woman with the typewriter and the man who made newspaper clippings were pegged as frontrunners.

It was the climax of Émile Cassel's documentary *The Shiverers*, which was the culmination of his postdoctoral research on that pleasurable tingling feeling triggered by very particular tactile noises, better known as ASMR. I was there because I was a finalist in a competitive ASMR tournament—in the Sans Props category—that provided the core narrative thrust for *The Shiverers*. The moment that I had realised I was about to catastrophically lose the tournament, the final round of the Props category was already well underway.

'Yrma.' Felix let the studio door shut softly and tiptoed to where I stood near the stencilled Ron Swanson. 'Are you okay?'

I smiled tepidly. 'Just nervous.'

He returned a smile that was partially obscured by his flourishing beard. This beard featured in many of his ASMR videos; he'd rub the wiry hairs against each other, or scurry his fingers across his jawline. There was some debate, before the commencement of the first heat, whether hair ought to count as a prop; Cassel ruled that for the purposes of the competition a prop was anything not naturally attached to one's body.

Felix kept a respectful distance from me as he leaned his back against the wall. He scratched his beard, not in the careful performative way of his ASMR videos, but because he had a genuine itch. 'Is this about Bella? It'll die down soon, I promise.'

Bella was the competitor that I defeated in the previous heat in order to secure my place in the final round. Despite the non-disclosure agreement, word about Bella's elimination had somehow reached her fanbase, an incensed subdivision of which was now flooding my videos with negative comments. *This is stupid*, they were saying. *I feel nothing*.

They weren't lying. My modest fame in ASMR circles was entirely accidental. It all came about because ever since I was a little girl I would suffer from mantras, as one might suffer from migraines. An inexplicably compelling phrase like *the net worth of Kim Kardashian West* would seize my head, bearing down on me with lacerating syllables, and the only relief was to record an internet video of myself repeating the mantra over and over, often in a clenched whisper, which turned out to be an unintentional ASMR trigger. It was my video of the mantra *David Mitchell the English comedian not the English novelist* that brought me to Cassel's attention, and led him to recruit me for his documentary.

But the thing was, the mantras would always lose power. I first observed this effect with my video of the mantra *Beyoncé's asymmetrical high-cut leotard and titanium roboglove*, which was popular for a very long time before it very suddenly was not doing anything for anyone, not even new listeners. It was not a consequence of the inevitable habituation to sensory triggers that requires ASMR fans to seek more and more videos; rather, it was an immediate and abrupt cessation of all effect.

And now, *George Gershwin's brother Ira*, I knew, no longer had power. I just knew. I was about to go into the studio and say a dead mantra into the microphone and look like a fool.

'Yrma? Don't worry about Bella. It'll be okay. She already released a video telling her fans to back off.'

'Thanks, Felix.' There was no point in conveying the truth to him. He clasped my shoulder and gave it a little squeeze. I thought, at least now, Felix might have a chance of winning: although many of the competitors were the softest and kindest examples of humanity, Felix was still my favourite.

We went back inside the studio to discover that, in something of an upset, the moisturising girl had won the Props category. Over the studio speakers, Cassel was replaying some of her victory-making triggers, which were literally just her rubbing moisturiser on her hands. Crew members were reconfiguring the stage for the Sans Props final, while the judges milled around the trestle tables which were set up for morning tea. Dark cables and wires pooled over and around the judges' abandoned chairs, as if this were the scene of a hostage escape.

'There you are.' Cassel's PA descended on Felix and me.

'We need you in the green room, please.'

The source and magnitude of Cassel's funding for *The Shiverers* remained one of the production's enduring mysteries. The parts of the documentary that concerned the tournament were all filmed in EBU's most modest studio, and yet Cassel seemed to command a sizeable variety of assistants, crew members, and equipment. Ayako, a sweet eighteen-year-old who was eliminated early in the competition and was renowned on YouTube for her artful manipulation of slime, used to joke that Cassel was in the pocket of Big ASMR, something we all appreciated, because if there were such a thing as Big ASMR then we had liked to imagine it was ruled by a wholesome bunch of somnambulant, fluffy bigwigs.

Felix and I allowed ourselves to be hustled into the green room for make-up touch-ups, and then hustled onstage to take our place in the row of black canvas chairs. At centre stage, there was a square card-table draped in black cloth, upon which sat the binaural microphone. There was also an adjustable piano stool for the active competitor.

The four judges had resumed their seats, and crew members were fitting them with the skin probes. These four judges were the actual protagonists of Cassel's documentary, the titular *Shiverers*; for the last nine months of shooting, Cassel had been studying their families and work lives, their sensations and desires, their determined pursuit of that purr of feeling rippling up scalp and spine. Unlike many of the other competitors, I thoroughly lacked any curiosity about our judges; although, when I performed in the previous rounds, I sometimes glimpsed clues to their lives underneath all those cables and probes—a medicine pouch clipped to a belt, model glue and paint crusted under fingernails, a wedding ring glinting on a hand curved attentively around a knee.

Judges, competitors, spectators, and crew affixed their wireless earbuds, and the Sans Props final began.

The first finalist, who I only knew by her YouTube handle ASMR Whisper Fairy, approached the microphone. She leaned close enough for us all to perceive the wet click of her lips parting. *'Hello, my lovelies,'* she whispered. *'How are we today?'*

She slowly twisted her lilac hair around one finger.

'I'm feeling ... a little bit sleepy today. But. Being here ... is really exciting. I've met ... so many lovely people ... during this competition. And I've felt really ... nice ... and ... tingly. Every day.'

Whisper Fairy continued like this, caressing her hair close to the microphone and breathing tremulously. Behind the judges, sensory monitors simmered with data that Cassel somehow interpreted to objectively determine a winner.

After Whisper Fairy came Anne, who had an elaborate personal attention routine where she roleplayed a college enrolment officer; then came Roger, who recited a recipe for cooking lamb shanks. On Felix's turn, he rummaged through his beard, made hollow popping sounds with his cheeks, rustled his hands and fingers together, scratched the bristles underneath his chin, and finished on a deep-throated hum.

Between each competitor, Cassel would jolt our ears with blasts of energetic pop music, which, as Whisper Fairy speculated in one of her early-round monologues, was '*kind of like how ... at perfume counters ... they have a bowl of coffee beans that you can sniff ... because the idea is that ... you need to cleanse your olfactory palate ... before smelling a new fragrance ... but you know, I heard, that actually ... sniffing bare, unfragranced skin is better.*'

And then, it was my turn. My throat was so dry as I took centre stage. I stalled for time by adjusting the height of the chair. In my periphery, Felix clasped his hands together and pumped them, smiling.

The mantra dropped into my head quite suddenly. The kettle bell force of it nearly snapped my neck, and I buckled at the waist. I gripped the edge of the card-table as if I were about to vomit. I said:

'*Ron Swanson's stencilled 'stache.*'

2. Sensory

You know what happened next. Soon enough I was running the world with *Ron Swanson's stencilled 'stache*. Cassel's documentary made it to Cannes and won the Palme d'Or. I released several videos of me saying *Ron Swanson's stencilled 'stache* while drinking cold-pressed juices, while demoing bright-coloured kitchen goods, while wearing ModCloth, while driving a Nissan Micra. I was flown to New York to meet Nick Offerman on the *Late Show with Stephen Colbert* and subsequently released an exclusive video of Nick Offerman and me taking turns saying *Ron Swanson's stencilled 'stache* which prompted a fierce bidding war between Netflix, Hulu, and Amazon Prime. I said *Ron Swanson's stencilled 'stache* in luxury boutique hotels and private golf clubs and before I presented the Academy Award for Best Sound Mixing; I wielded giant novelty scissors and presented giant novelty cheques. Doors that were previously closed to me—and that I didn't even know were doors—were now open, held wide by chiselled men in tight polo shirts and minted smiles.

And throughout it all, although I always feared the day would come, *Ron Swanson's stencilled 'stache* never lost power. The mantra stayed firmly embedded in my head as if it were hand-carved there by Ron Swanson himself. If I was suspicious before that the compelling nature of the mantras actually had nothing to do with ASMR and was a phenomenon completely unto itself—some kind of sublime consensus between time, speaker, and phrase—then I was fully convinced now. I was shouting and spitting and howling *Ron Swanson's stencilled 'stache* and it had whatever effect the listener thought it should have.

'Do you ever want to say other things?' asked Felix when I was visiting him in New Zealand. He was the only person who ever asked me that.

'No,' I said. 'It is literally the only thing that I want to say. Not even "want to". Must. I must keep saying the mantra until there is a new mantra.'

'Who encouraged you to start making videos in the first place, anyway?'

And disquietingly, I could not remember. Or rather, it was a question that did not have an answer that was capable of being remembered. It was like asking a dancer, why do you dance?

More disquieting incidents followed. I was invited to give the opening night speech at an exhibition in MoMA. After *Ron Swanson's stencilled 'stache*–ing the crowd I took some time to explore the gallery. One installation consisted of a set of headphones hanging from a nail in a dark booth, and when you picked up the headphones and listened, you'd hear a looped recording of the artist going, '*Hey … could you not … murmur … could you not … murmur … like, could you not?*' Except, when I listened to it, I was convinced the artist was saying *Yrma*, and was speaking directly to me. *Yrma. Could you not?*

Then, I was invited to sing the national anthem at the Australian Open before a Federer–Nadal match. The glass bottle of Spring Valley mango and banana nectar in my sponsors' gift basket yielded this 'liddle fact' printed on the underside of the green bottlecap: *No. 804: You need to stop.*

And then, when I was in Venice for a celebration of Antonio Vivaldi, a nimble plane looped a message in the sky—*S T O P I T*—and it took the entire gondola ride for the letters to finally disperse.

Each time I encountered a message that implored me to stop what I was doing, the sensations in my body were the unholy cousins of ASMR: a stomach-falling-through-a-trap-door feeling, the numb impotence of a syringe plunged into a vein, and, the worst of them, that feeling of a thread of hair stuck in your mouth that you can't seem to tongue away. On the occasions when the sensations were so bad I couldn't sleep, I tried immersing myself in Felix's Bedtime Tingles videos and Ayako's slime videos, but because they were my fellow competitors in Cassel's tournament and thus reminders of how I came to be in this very predicament, I would lie awake in the cold indigo light, nerve-bitten, twitching, strapped hopelessly to consciousness like half an avocado to one of those avocado saver things.

The terrible thing was that I did not want to stop. My life had reached an apex of cool perfection; I was more loved than ever. In my life before *Ron Swanson's stencilled 'stache*, I was not like Whisper Fairy or Bella or Ayako, with their porcelain cuticles and subtle pores; I lacked their grace and gentleness and general aura of competence. I was unaccustomed to the niceness that their personae seemed to call forth in others, of which *Ron Swanson's stencilled 'stache* had permitted me the briefest taste.

I wasn't sure, either, *how* I could bring it all to a stop. My inbox was stacked with offers and opportunities. The notion of extricating myself from the elaborate pyramid of endorsements, Q&As, editorials, audiobooks, exclusive web content, children's hospital visits, pop-culture conventions, academic conferences, voice cameos, and reality TV guest judge appearances seemed not only impossible to action, but deeply embarrassing.

So it took a well-composed email from a fan—asking me to give my blessing to a *Ron Swanson's stencilled 'stache* tattoo stencil, and hoping that I didn't mind Felix passing on my email address—to draw me into a crowded Pret A Manger in Greenwich on a mid-week morning.

I was desperately blotting at a spot of coffee that I had splashed on myself when he crash-landed into the seat opposite me: a middle-aged man, navy blue hoodie with the sleeves rolled up to the knobs of his elbows, yellow baseball cap jammed over his distraught ginger hair. He spoke immediately: 'Listen, Yrma, I lied to you, I don't know Felix, my name is Allan and I'm here to tell you to stop, listen, you have to stop.'

'Allan?' I echoed, still mid-blot, crumpling the wet napkin in my hand.

'Yes, Allan, and listen'—he pulled his baseball cap more snugly over his head—'I really need you to stop. You haven't listened to my other messages.'

His other messages? '*You're* the one who set up the MoMA installation,' I gasped. '*You* put the "liddle fact" in my mango and banana nectar. *You* were behind the skywriting in Venice.'

'Yes, that's right—'

'Wow, that all must've been very difficult to set up.'

'Yes, they were *very* difficult to set up.' He sounded extremely cross when he said this, but—and I wasn't sure if I imagined it—he also sounded thrilled.

'I'm sorry,' I said. 'I don't know what to tell you. I need this. I *need* to keep saying *Ron Swanson's sten*—'

'Stop!' he yelped. His fingers flew up to his face.

And I did stop, because I recognised that look, that grimace, the little rupture lines of pain. 'Do you suffer from mantras too?' I blurted out.

'What?'

'*Ron Swanson*, it's a mantra, you see, it gets stuck in my head and—'

'No, no-no-no. I'm—' He fumbled. 'I'm. It's. Do you know. Are you familiar with post-hypnotic suggestion?'

'What?'

'It's my trigger phrase,' he said. 'You keep saying my trigger phrase and I don't want to go back.'

He pulled on the peak of his cap again, half stood up and sat down, and finally snatched my glass of water and gulped it all before I could tell him that I'd previously dipped my napkin in it.

'I don't understand,' I said. 'Who *are* you?'

'I'm.' He put the glass back on the table too emphatically so that it toppled; he scrambled to upright it. 'I'm. I guess you could say I'm a sort of … agent.'

'A secret agent?'

'Yes, but.' He licked his lips. 'I don't want to go back, see? I don't want to.'

'What do you mean, "go back"?'

'To my *employers*.'

'Who are your employers? Who do you work for?'

'I can't *tell you that*. The point is, Yrma, please, you have to *stop*.'

'I've been saying *Ron Swanson's*—'

'Don't!'

'... I've been saying *the mantra* for months and months now. Why should I just—you're asking me to—'

'Stop it. Please. It does something to me.'

'It does something to *me*,' I said. 'I can't *help* it.'

He stared at me. 'So you're with them?'

'What?'

'Do you work for *them*?'

'I don't work for anybody! I just—the mantra comes. And I say it. To my subscribers. Until I don't need to say it anymore. And it just so happens that *this* mantra has, well, taken off, I guess, in a way that the others haven't.'

His wristwatch clamoured, a bright panic of beeps. Allan staggered out of his chair—'I have to—I can't stay—*please*—'

He tumbled into the aisle and bolted, stymied momentarily by the Push/Pull glass doors, and then flung himself into the street.

I sat there, flabbergasted, ears ringing, still clutching the napkin. I peeled myself from the chair and weaved out of the

Pret A Manger, into the hazy Greenwich morning, immediately in other pedestrians' way—looked left and right but could not see Allan's skedaddling form.

'*Yrma Le Guin follow me DON'T LOOK AT ME JUST WALK.*'

Vice grip at the elbow, shunting me into a brisk gait.

3. Meridian

'*Don't look at me JUST WALK.*'

'I'm walking,' I bleated, stumbling over my feet. I caught a glimpse of the tightly knotted sash of a trenchcoat and red-soled Louboutins walking at a menacing clip.

'You just met Allan McKenzie, did you not?'

'Yeah, I guess I did—'

'*Don't look at me just walk.*' Flanked by another trenchcoat, this one in sharp leather lace-ups and argyle socks.

'So you are aware that Allan McKenzie is a rogue asset that you must bring to heel immediately.'

'Me? Why—'

'Don't pretend you don't know.'

'I *really* don't.'

'You've been playing along for years.'

'No I haven't!'

'*Your videos,*' the left trenchcoat hissed.

'My mantras?'

'They are not *your* mantras, they are *ours*, and they are not *mantras*, they are *very important codes*, and *you* are messing it all up.'

'*You've* been sending me these mantras? *How?*'

'And it's *wrong*; it's not that nonsense about Ron Swanson, it's *John Johnson's fended stash.*'

'Who's John Johnson?'

'Millennials,' sighed the left-hand trenchcoat.

Both of my captors had some kind of scout patch stitched into their trenchcoats, but I could only make out the one on my right in any detail. It appeared to depict a snake twining itself through a ladder, and the words: *Our machinations are disturbingly lively.*

The right-hand trenchcoat renewed her grip on my elbow and *don't-look-at-me-JUST-WALK*'d me again.

My stomach somersaulted when I realised where they were frogmarching me: Greenwich Park, the site of a massive public celebration of the birthday of the youngest Mountbatten-Windsor, which was already in full swing. I had recently turned down an invitation to speak there because I had ascertained that the event was either unauthorised or reluctantly authorised.

Giant flatscreens had been erected like extravagant portals, displaying live footage from the Mountbatten-Windsor's actual birthday party in France. People could have their picture taken with a variety of giant cardboard cutouts of the royal family, some as individuals and some conjoined in formal sittings. Food carts hawked Bucking-Ham Sandwiches and Baron Carrot-Fig-Us Cake.

'You're going to get up there,' the left-hand trenchcoat growled, slicing a hand at the small community stage, 'and say *John Johnson's fended stash.*'

'No,' I hissed. 'You say it.'

The right-hand trenchcoat yanked me towards the stage. 'It has to be you.'

'Why?'

'McKenzie will only respond to you.'

'What kind of agency *are* you? This is, like, stunningly impractical.'

'Yes, exactly,' she exclaimed in a *so-you-get-it!* way. 'Stunning.'

'Stunning,' the left-hand trenchcoat agreed. They seemed to share the same cross-and-thrilled aura as Allan McKenzie.

I wriggled out of their grip. 'This is ridiculous. I'm not doing this!'

'We thought so.' The left-hand trenchcoat held up his phone screen in front of my face. It took me a while to make sense of what I was looking at.

'Feelgood Felix ASMR.'

'Yes.'

Felix's YouTube channel had been reduced to a single video. The left-hand trenchcoat thumbed the play command. Felix was standing at his binaural microphone, touching his beard, but then all of a sudden he stopped, pivoted, hands still curled underneath his chin. My captors stepped into frame, and then the video blinked out.

'And don't even try *Ron Swanson's stencilled 'stache*–ing us,' the right-hand trenchcoat said. 'It will only make us *exceptionally less agreeable.*'

They knew they had me. The left-hand trenchcoat gave me a little shove and I stumbled towards the stage. I climbed the steps, trembling, while all around me the screens radiated posh smiles and couture. I walked to the lectern and bent the microphone. It crackled to life obligingly, and while all around the park exuberant Britons munched Eliza-beef Pies and snapped selfies with an outdated cardboard Meghan-and-Harry, the crowd directly in front of me became still. A mum leaned down to her daughter and said, 'Look!'

'H-hello,' I stammered, fixing the microphone again. My voice seemed to be amplified throughout the entire park. I glanced at my captors. The left-hand trenchcoat waggled his phone at me.

What was the correct mantra again? 'J-John. *John Johnson's*—'

The screens snapped to black. I managed to say *fended stash* but my microphone dropped out. When the screens were revived, I saw a giant pair of hands with luminous pink nails, and—blurrily in the background, cut off at the chin—the owner of the luminous pink nails: a teenager in a pearl-coloured sweater. She rubbed her fingers together slowly, making a pleasant rustling sound not unlike the beginning of rain.

She reached to the side and swivelled the pink pump head of a 1.5L bottle of moisturising cream. She sank her hand down on the pump. The cream came out thick and indulgent and glistening. She let the coin-sized dollop sit in her flat palm, and brought the other palm over it. She rubbed them together in opposing circular motions.

The effect on the crowd was mixed. Some succumbed to a hushed calm; others giggled; a child said, 'What the HELL is this?'

But the effect on the trenchcoats was singular. They clutched their heads just like I used to when I was tormented by mantras. 'Aur-gha-gh!' they groaned. The one with the Louboutins teetered out of her shoes; the other dropped his phone in the grass. They bumped into each other and wailed. Completely disarmed, flushed of their former power, like pimples hollowed of pus.

'Yrma,' said a voice behind me. 'Quick! Come with us.'

I only had time to register the whip of a blonde ponytail as the speaker jumped off the stage and darted behind a hedge. The flatscreens were still projecting the moisturising girl, who was working the cream in-between her fingers. She was really getting into the webbing. I couldn't see the trenchcoats anymore, and someone in the crowd was trying to get some applause going for some reason. I ducked off the stage and threw myself behind the hedge.

'This way,' said a new voice. A hand laid on my wrist: fingernails crusted with model glue and paint. I allowed myself to be pulled a little way, as we were joined by others hurrying away from the scene. The paint-stained hand slipped off my wrist as we broke into a jog. I swear I saw Anne the college enrolment officer roleplayer running ahead of me.

I escaped with my apparent conspirators to a cemetery, where everyone seemed to be congratulating and hugging each other. The girl with the blonde ponytail stood with her hands on her hips in an approving manner, unsmiling but proud. 'Did you do all that?' I asked her. 'With the screens and everything?'

'That's right! You don't have to worry about those weird dudes any more, Yrma! Just keep doing what you do! And don't worry about Felix either. My people have him now.'

'Who *are* you guys?' I stared bleary-eyed around the cemetery. People were already dispersing, not as rapidly as a flash mob, but with enough purpose and vigour that it was clear they weren't interested in staying around and chatting.

'We're the global self-appointed representatives of ASMR YouTubers, such as yourself, as well as ASMR enthusiasts and enthusiasts who have yet to discover the term ASMR, as well as researchers in ASMR such as Émile Cassel, and a variety of incorporated and unincorporated entities that wish to monetise ASMR. We also represent insomniacs, sensitive and pure types, and people who just want to relax. In other words,' she said, 'we're Big ASMR.'

My body was a host to all sorts of new sensations then, the most dominant of which was a peculiar chill that was both comforting and foreboding. The girl with the ponytail glanced around me to issue a succinct wave to one of her co-conspirators.

'So,' I said. 'So. Have you known the whole time about my mantras being ... post-hypnotic triggers to a legion of secret agents?'

'Oh yeah,' the girl said blithely. 'We intervened. Hijacked your signal, as it were. That Ron Swanson stencil graffiti at EBU? We put that there.'

I thought of that judge with the model glue and paint stains, and the ingenuity and resourcefulness and fucking craftiness of the ASMR videomakers in general.

'Worked way better than we thought,' the girl chuckled, squinting fondly at the memory.

'But why?' I asked.

The girl tilted her head.

'What was this all *for?*'

'Hey, Yrma,' the girl said. 'Everyone's just chasing a thrill, you get it? Allan McKenzie, those trenchcoat weirdos, that whole ridiculous snake-and-ladder agency. Devoting their lives to constructing the exact circumstances that will permit their own specific and singular release. Despite our philo-sophical differences—*their* humourless, complicated plots; *our* penchant for undermining them—you, me, McKenzie and the rest: we're all wired for *some* kind of thrill. Our proclivities take on a life of their own. You know what they say. *Our machinations are disturbingly lively.* I hope you keep making your videos.'

She turned to walk away, but before she did, she twisted her head to meet my eye. '*Maddox, Pax, Zahara,*' she said. '*Shiloh, Knox, and Vivienne.*'

One of my old mantras—from two, three years ago. That video wasn't even on YouTube anymore. The girl slipped away, and a giant cheer erupted from the festival area of the park, as the crowd began to sing as one: '*Happy Birthday to you ...*'

4. Response

The pigment of the stencilled Ron Swanson at Erdős-Bacon University was still as dark and crisp as I remembered it, still exuding Ron Swanson's special kind of insouciant gravitas from the design's negative spaces. On a Sunday, the campus was dewy and peaceful; distantly, I heard the whistle of an umpire, the smack of a penalty kick, and my head, for once, was as unblemished as the sky.

Felix was coming across the car park, hands so deep and flat in his pockets that his shoulders seemed fixed in a defensive shrug—I almost tumbled into a profusion of apologies, again, for his short-lived kidnapping. But then as he drew nearer, he lifted his head and smiled for me, that furry familiar smile, and I found that I could smile back.

'Thanks for meeting me here,' I said.

'Well,' he said, 'you paid for my plane ticket.'

'Yeah, well … I don't think I'll be able to do that for you again anytime soon.'

After that day in Greenwich, I did not *Ron Swanson's stencilled 'stache* again. The same magic that propelled me to stardom also, it seemed, gently spooled me back into anonymity. I released a new video that morning—*Hillary Clinton's pocketless pantsuit*—and it had only twenty-one views so far, but that was okay with me.

Felix stood up straight, pinned his legs and feet together. 'Ready?'

'Yeah.'

I stooped on the gravel and used the edge of a key to remove the lid of the paint can. Felix dropped to his haunches and helped me lift and tip the can, letting the paint cascade thickly into the plastic tray. We only had one roller, so I watched as Felix trundled it back and forth through the paint. He let me have a go at it too. It was quite soothing.

Before Felix laid the first stripe of paint, I touched the stencilled Ron Swanson, tenderly and respectfully, as if it were an ancient glyph. I stood on tippy-toe. I kissed Ron Swanson's stencilled 'stache. Then nodded at Felix, who began to roll.

WASHING DAY

What Kate misses the most these days is the 'vintage inspired' smock dress she bought from ASOS. It had the appearance of being made up of several different cuts of material, like a patchwork, but it was actually all just one piece of fabric, a simulated bricolage of floral prints in pink, indigo, blue—but predominantly red, so she wore it to the Lunar New Year gathering the last time she went home. The waistline sat a bit higher than in a regular dress—just below her bust—which had a welcome obfuscating effect on the rest of her body, transforming the slack geography of her torso into a floaty hypothetical world, inscrutable to tactless relatives. She could wear the dress with black tights in cold weather, with Doc Martens, with flats, with high heels; its lightness was ideal for both the dry heat of Australia and the humidity of Singapore. And: it had pockets.

Sometimes, even now, she reaches into her wardrobe to

find it—perhaps, all this time, it was just a prank between the wardrobe and the washing machine—and she won't find it, won't find it in her jungle of a clothes rack either, or in the laundry hamper, and she'll feel the tight hand of grief, followed by a swipe of admonishment. They're just clothes.

It happened in the year that Kate turned thirty. She had just returned from her second ever Booty Burn class, glazed with sweat and embarrassment. When she peeled off her crop top and workout pants she discovered that the elastic had scored red lines into her skin, as if she were an animal in a butcher's diagram. After taking a shower and wriggling into sweatpants and T-shirt, she bundled up the crop top and workout pants together with the rest of the clothes in the laundry hamper (separating the 'vintage inspired' smock dress into its own mesh bag), piled everything into the washing machine, and clicked the dial to a gentle cold cycle.

It's not that the women at the Booty Burn class were mean or snobby. It's not that they were intimidating—although, Kate *was* intimidated: by thighs that were tauter and longer than hers, neatly parcelled abdomens, shapely curled brackets of collarbones. And sitting there on the polished studio floor before class began, trying to tell herself that these women weren't trying to be thin and beautiful *at* her, she realised that the itching nervous silence wasn't just emanating from her. During the class, the women lunged, flexed, curled, stretched—gazes fixed and earnest—balanced on private cliffs of worry, projected back to them in the mirrored studio wall.

And it's not like Vanessa, the Booty Burn instructor, was mean or snobby either. She was younger than most of the women in the class, probably only a few years out of high school. She looked the part of a fitness instructor, fitted sleekly in her black workout pants with diamond-shaped mesh cut-outs and white singlet knotted sharply at the midriff, but her voice was incongruously light, rising above the frantic fitness music not with volume but more in the way of the glassy notes of a harp. She kept saying things like *honour your body*, and *breathe through the shape*, and *if it's available to you, take it to a jump*.

This last phrase Kate found interesting. *If it's available to you, peel your heels off the floor. If it's available to you, extend your legs to a full plank. If this is not available to you today, come down to your forearms or knees.* She wondered if she could begin to think of her daily efforts as dependent on the shifting availabilities of her body. She massaged the red lines intersecting her torso and tried to love and understand and honour her body into something less conspicuous, something to carry without apology.

She was still pondering this idea when the washing machine carolled its end-of-cycle song. She slid the laundry basket from the shelf, unfolded its legs, set it down beside the machine. The countdown display was blinking '00.00'. She lifted the lid.

Would she have heard it, if she'd listened closely?

Perhaps, as it accelerated towards the final spin, the machine groaned with less effort than usual; perhaps, the timbre of its hum was mischievously lighter. Perhaps, as the last pirouettes forfeited momentum, a careful listener would have noticed the absence of damp clothes slapping against the drum.

Or perhaps, the crucial moment occurred at some other time, in-between the washing machine's bright waking-up notes and the inhale of the lifted lid. Maybe as water filled the chamber, maybe as the agitator made its first twists, maybe as the suds were purged before the rinse cycle. Maybe it happened gradually—first one sock, then a pair of briefs, then a singlet, then a blouse. Pantyhose slurped up like a noodle, one leg at a time; the last percussive grasp of a zipper, a button, the Working With Children ID badge she neglected to unfasten from her work shirt.

Or perhaps there was no way of knowing, no way of catching on before it was too late. Perhaps it was a Schrödinger-esque paradox: the clothes were simultaneously swirling like fish in the gut of the machine, and they were swirling somewhere else.

It was unclear who should have been in charge of investigating the anomaly. At first, people were phoning the police, suspecting theft or trickery. Manufacturers' helplines bloated with calls. Newsfeeds rippled with perplexed status updates, snapshots of washing machines standing empty and gape-mouthed. And then—once the trend became clear—videos captured on mobile phones.

It was always the case, even with the frontloaders, that you could never discern the exact moment when the clothes disappeared.

By the time the Physics department of the University of Sydney became the official hub of investigative efforts, the weekend had elapsed. No one could replicate the results of the fateful day. Clothes went in, clothes came out. No matter the variation: warm or cold water, spin or no spin, Whirlpool, LG, Fisher & Paykel. The anomaly was limited to that single day, in this single country. The opportunity to study the anomaly was gone.

Her tartan shawl. Her Totoro socks.

Four pairs of her favourite underwear, a discontinued boyleg style from Target, with the lace waistbands that didn't pinch the skin around her stomach and hips.

A green tunic top that flared slightly into a handkerchief hemline, long enough to cover her bottom.

A flesh-coloured bra with cups that were just the right shape and height that they could nestle invisibly underneath a spaghetti-strap top.

A pair of jeggings that she acquired before jeggings became popular—more like denim tights—that forewent the insulting fake pockets and were thick enough to hide underwear seams.

A black office skirt. A grey T-shirt.

A hoodie with thumbholes in the sleeves.

A dress printed with bees.

Denim shorts made soft by years of wear.

A week after the anomaly she was back at Booty Burn class, constantly pulling down on her tank top in case her underwear lines were showing (something she didn't have to worry about until those boyleg briefs were surrendered to the anomaly).

Before the class started, there was some chatter among the women about their missing laundry. Miranda had lost all of her good bed linen. Amy, her most comfortable pair of maternity trousers. The navy blue formal shirt with square gold buttons that Karen bought for her husband. Glenda's daughter's favourite *Star Wars* pyjamas. At Helen's children's school, the principal had relaxed the dress rules for students on account of all the school uniforms that vanished in the wash. 'It's the same at my kids' school,' said Una, and then burst into tears, because, 'It'll cost so much to replace those uniforms. Even the secondhand ones aren't cheap. And they just grow out of them. They just grow out of them.' Francine, luckily, did her washing on a weekday, but, 'My boyfriend couldn't resist giving it a go, and now he has to replace all his jocks.'

Kate listened, but could not bring herself to join in. It was somehow not available to her, to speak, standing there in her hurriedly purchased workout pants, stiff and new. Though she was sure these women would understand—they *would*—the strange heartbreak of it all.

The day after the anomaly, her mother had called from Singapore. 'Katie, did you read the email I sent you? Don't wash your clothes, okay? Did you read the email?'

Yes, she did, but it was too late—and besides, the anomaly was over. People were doing their laundry just fine now.

'Okay, but be careful! Don't wash anything important. Try putting a few things first, like towels, but not your good ones, just one or two things at a time like that, okay? Do you need me to send clothes? If you want, I send clothes? Do you have enough panties? Don't buy, I can send things.'

She told her mother that the clothes she missed the most were irreplaceable. Like the dress she wore at Lunar New Year, remember.

'Ah, don't worry—you'll find other dresses.'

At work, Kate's breath would stall in her throat if she saw a child scrunch away their jacket or lunchbox or favourite stuffed toy into their backpack. Something about the darkness of the backpack's depths, the finality of the zipper's joined teeth. As if one could now never be sure whether a vessel can be trusted to guard the things that it holds.

'Bellybutton to spine,' Vanessa reminded the class. 'Work from your core.'

There were theories, of course. A dirty alliance between whitegoods manufacturers and the fashion industry. A bizarre punishment meted out by the Water Corporation to people who activated their sprinklers on the wrong days. A stunt engineered by Facebook, maybe even by Mark Zuckerberg himself.

The academics tasked with the investigation examined all the available footage, made house visits, placed pushpins on maps. But what was the true scope of data that they were meant to collect? What else could possibly be relevant? Should they have looked at the position of the moon on the date of the anomaly, or the UV index? Wind conditions? Should they have multiplied the date by pi? Hunted for a butterfly on the exact opposite side of the globe, reprogramming the universe with the binary beats of its wings?

The Prime Minister made an awkward lunge for relatability—the day of the anomaly was laundry day in his household, too—but all he got for his trouble was public interest in who *does* the laundry at The Lodge, and how did the PM divide household chores before he moved into The Lodge, and has the PM ever done a load of laundry himself?

Certain corners of the internet nurtured a theory that it

was all a feminist conspiracy, some petulant and humiliating revenge against hardworking husbands and fathers. Their work shirts and footy jerseys were hostages to an organised temper tantrum, and they'll turn up in time once the wives and girlfriends unknot their knickers and accept that this is just the way things are, not being sexist or anything, but women are just better at stuff like this; 'course, bit of a mixed message, the women hiding their own clothes too, but maybe it's a ploy to update their wardrobes, you know how they are.

You'll find other dresses. But what Kate's mother doesn't appreciate is that Kate's wardrobe is full of *other dresses*— dresses that Kate has grown out of but can't let go, dresses that changed size or shape in the wash, dresses worn only once. Dresses with elastic waists that constantly wriggle up underneath her breasts, dresses with straps that fall off her shoulders, dresses that exact an overbearing grip on her upper arms. Dresses with gaping V-necks, dresses rendered tacky from pilling, dresses with vexed buttonholes. Dresses that haven't kept their promises. Dresses that, like ex-lovers, she feels foolish for ever feeling worthy of.

Is it a memory, or a nightmare? Kate, eight years old, walking home from school, to the block of HDB flats where her family lived. Someone's bamboo washing pole had dislodged from the socket; there were clothes flattened on the footpath, as if a whole family had just melted there. 'Not ours, please not ours,' Kate murmured, getting closer and closer, heart sinking with each garment she recognised—her mother's oversized Garfield sleep tee, her father's polo shirt with the tiny palm-tree print, Kate's orange corduroy pinafore. There were two uncles playing chess on the void deck, and plenty more kids arriving home from school, so she tried to appear nonchalant as she approached the fallen pole, coming to kneel before the crumpled clothes. The clothes were dry on their exposed faces but still damp in the creases. Her mind bloomed with what ifs:

What if the clothes have been lying here all day?

What if the pole hit someone on the way down?

What if it made a loud noise when it landed?

What if everyone came out to look at it? The grandma on the fourth floor who tended sagging pot plants? The bristly uncle who always scolded children for running? The slick-bunned businesswoman whose high-heel clip echoed through the complex as she took the elevator to level three and walked up the stairwell to level four? The twin boys who lived directly above Kate's home who were always screaming?

What if they gathered around the fallen pole? Sifted through the clothes like they were suspiciously low-priced goods in a discount bin, picking up this garment and that garment between pinched fingers? Or what if they just walked around it, *tsk-tsk*-ing under their breaths? Or maybe they approached it as Kate did—*not mine, please not mine*—and, doused with relief at the sight of an unfamiliar shirt, a dress of the wrong size, continued briskly on their way?

Kate bundled up all the clothes and smuggled them back to the apartment. She left the pole for her father to fetch later. And she doesn't remember ever wearing the orange pinafore after that.

It was common, following the anomaly, for people to replace their toploaders with frontloaders, just for that extra imagined security of having a front-facing window to one's laundry. Large cardboard boxes began to appear at the childcare centre, donated by parents, and Kate and her co-workers would help the children repurpose the boxes into trucks and forts and spaceships. One child insisted that her cardboard box be turned into a washing machine.

'Are you sure?' Kate asked the child. 'This box can be anything, you know. It can be a ship. A robot. A castle.'

'No. Definitely a washing machine.' The child, Sasha, gave a firm nod.

So Kate used a Stanley knife to cut a round hole in the box, and a larger incomplete circle around that to create a door that could pop outwards, and a smaller flap in the top corner for the powder dispenser. She attached milk bottle lids with split pins to form the dials. Sasha drew on a digital display with a felt-tip marker, and also an energy rating of five stars.

'Shall we test it out? Should we wash some clothes?' Kate

asked once Sasha announced that it was finished.

'I want to be clothes,' Sasha said.

So Kate opened the door and Sasha climbed in. She pivoted so that she was looking at Kate through the window, squatting on her haunches. Kate closed the door and poised her hand over the dials. 'Do you want a warm wash or a cold wash?'

'Cold!'

'Delicate or heavy duty?'

'Heavy duty!'

'Okay, I'm pressing the start button,' Kate said. 'What sound does a washing machine make when it's filling up with water?'

'*Shhhhhhhhhhhhhhhh,*' went Sasha. '*Shhhhhhhhhhhaaaaaaaaaaaaaaaaaaaahhhhhhhh.*'

In her own time, Sasha morphed the sound into a *whom-whom-whom-whom-whom-whom-whom* and shuffled around so she was side-on to the window. She placed her palms on the box floor and dipped her head and rolled over in a tight somersault, over and over again, an ecstatic blur of hair and overalls and limbs.

Over the hour of playtime, other children took turns inside Sasha's machine. They'd climb in one, two, even three at a time, tumbling over and around each other to the hum of their kaleidoscopic onomatopoeia. The bottle cap dials began to control other things, like speed or noise or gravity or smell. Kate let herself recede into the background of their play. She watched the washing machine become another thing, and another thing, and another thing, the children's imaginations as agile as their bodies. A washing machine can be a ticket booth. A time travel machine. An aeroplane.

A hovercraft. A bank vault.

An aquarium. An escape pod.

A doomsday weapon.

A teleportation device.

Today is washing day. Today is the fiftieth washing day since the anomaly. Kate opens the cane lid of the laundry hamper. She hooks the clasps of her bras and tucks them into a mesh bag. She checks her pockets for tissues. She turns her printed shirts inside-out. She un-concertinas her socks. She sprays the armpits of her work shirts with stain remover. She closes the lid. Wakes up the machine. Twists the dial to a gentle wash.

The countdown displays '0.51'.

Entreats her approval with a steady blink.

What if, on this fiftieth time, she were to climb into the washing machine? Inhale bellybutton to spine, dip one leg first and then the other, wrap her torso around the agitator, reach up to jostle the lid until it tips shut? What if, today, it is finally available to her to do so—to make herself into the necessary shape, to be the perfect fit?

Kate pushes the start button. The washing machine accumulates water, grows in noise and intensity and purpose—as if it means to ascend, as if ascension is indeed available to it—while one minute drops from the countdown, and then another, and then another.

YES! YES! YES YOU ARE! YES YOU ARE!

Philip Glass says there's a full moon rising, three days from now, and we can't wait for Boots any longer—she's gone to the whitecoats and been injected with death. Tybalt confirmed it: the burial of Boots, wrapped in a blanket and covered in dirt, the family's youngest child sobbing. Boots was our best—all the bells in the world couldn't stop her from ripping heart from wing—and that's probably why they took her to the whitecoats: she was entirely too talented a killer, too sufficient, feline to the core. She would rather eat grasshoppers than kibble.

Philip Glass reminds us that we are all of us worthy, we are all of us clawed and feline-witted, but sometimes Philip Glass is overly optimistic, and we miss Boots.

Then someone starts calling for Dumpling and we have to

disperse, melting over the trees and fences, everywhere smelling of children and smoke, the vibrations of school buses, the sunny paths dotted with parents escorting their babies safely home.

When Philip Glass and I get back, the lady's first student for the day has already arrived, the one with the wobbly tempo, so I sleep at the other end of the house while Philip Glass patrols the wall outside.

We were purchased together, Philip Glass and I. It was the lady who gave us our tags. I think we have grown into the shape of them, just as we have grown into the shape of her life. The lady's only visitors are her students and their parents; our afternoons are filled with shuffling cars and doors, tedious songs, high-pitched small talk. Sometimes a child will ask to see Philip Glass or me, but these days Philip Glass will always be outside, on his endless patrol, and so it will fall on me to be sociable. The lady and the child will crouch nearby and say, 'O Fortuna, O Fortuna,' and make clicking lip sounds, and, if the mood takes me, I will crawl out from my hiding place and let the child inexpertly rub my spine, little hands smelling of varnish and perspiration, sticky as only children can be. Sometimes I do not acknowledge them—sometimes I do not quite see them properly, as if they inhabit a slanted universe, only slightly intersecting the one that I live in.

I dream of green fluorescent water, of the full moon rising. Of Boots, all that clever muscle, wasting under the earth.

Three days, Philip Glass said—and he is never wrong.

Dumpling's is the best place for our meetings; the house and the surrounding walls are full of difficult angles that obscure the back lawn, and everywhere there is junk—old tyres, rusted washing machines. The house is cluttered with young people who read discoloured paperbacks and smoke on the front steps. We like to gather around two o'clock, arriving little by little, taking up our positions. For the longest time, we don't speak at all; we notice, and don't notice, the others. Eventually Philip Glass, who always has the highest vantage point—on top of the shed, usually, or the ledge of the bathroom window—will make an observation or pronouncement that will cause the others to flicker, that will draw us once again into the same universe.

Right now, Philip Glass says that there's a house on Wood Street that might have some new blood. Tybalt reported a moving truck yesterday morning. He didn't see the cats themselves, but he saw the movers unloading a baroque procession of interlocking scratching posts, fuzzed with old claw marks, pungent with hair and saliva. Maybe two cats, Tybalt suggests, and then finds something in his hair that must be licked out immediately.

Always coming in twos these days, Kupo says.

It's because it's the same price to purchase two cats—Philip Glass and O Fortuna are the same, Dumpling says.

They're young, then?

Not necessarily, Philip Glass says. It goes: kittens, most expensive. Adolescents, moderately expensive. Old cats, least expensive. But, no matter what, if two are purchased, only the price of one is paid.

But why?

Nobody is quite sure how to answer. Kupo is always full of these plaintive questions. I'm thinking about something Boots once said: the only way any animal can win is to make more animals. It's the thing your oppressors are always most afraid of—that there will be more of you than there are of them—and that's all the more reason to do it. Outfuck the enemy.

Boots mothered two litters of children before they managed to sterilise her for good.

We have drifted from the point again. Dumpling is tracking a cicada through the dying grass. Kupo dozes. And Philip Glass stares out over the yard, ears swivelling to follow passing vehicles, so alert that he is barely present.

But then we all feel the chill at the same time. As if the sun has passed behind a cloud and been replaced by another celestial body, a copy of the real sun. The smell of chlorine.

Two days.

The new blood, I say. On Wood Street. I can investigate. See what they're like.

Tybalt emerges from his coat. I can come, he says. I know which house it is.

Very good then, says Philip Glass.

Tybalt leads me to the new household on Wood Street. There are no cars in the driveway and no scent of cats. They'll be staying indoors, Tybalt says. While they're new.

At first I don't know if Tybalt is going to follow me. I squeeze under the gap in the gate into a narrow corridor between the neighbouring fence and the lounge room windows, a path covered in pebbles. There are spiny, uncomfortable plants clustered against the fence. Through the twin grey windows I can see a small neighbourhood of brown boxes, some of which have been slit open and partially unloaded. The structure of interlocking scratching posts is the only thing completely assembled, but it is empty. Imitation mice dangle from pieces of string.

Tybalt has decided to follow me after all. He sniffs the tip of one of the plants and tries to rub against it. Wood Street is close to the main road, and far from Tybalt's house: he would have had to have been let out of the house very early in order to witness the moving van. But Tybalt has a way of witnessing a great many things. Catching the scent of news on the wind.

I turn back to the grey windows, and—

Two cats. One at each window. Hunched, unblinking.

And then everyone's hackles are up. The blacks of our eyes thicken, and a yowl bubbles in the female's throat, but it seems that everybody intends to outlast the others in stillness, nobody willing even to exhale. Our coats are the only things that move, hairs lengthening, as if blood rises to the tips.

We stay locked like this for several minutes. I introduce myself and Tybalt, and then we spend several minutes more bristling. The cats are brother and sister, adult but undersized, and already I can intuit their story—a sick mother with sickly children, shivering and slimy in a ditch; they were probably pegged as goners. But Philip Glass will accept anybody, even sick cats on special diets, so I ask:

Do you smell chlorine at dusk?

Do you dream of glowing water?

Do you see the waxing moon?

These questions are enough to unite us. Slowly we steady ourselves, draw our coats back to our bodies. We stare at each other until we are almost bored. Eventually, the brother licks his maw, lifts his hind leg above his head, and begins to wash.

The sister says: For two days and two nights we have not seen the sky. We have not touched our noses to the grass. And yet, we recognise it: the smell of death. You do not need to ask us, for we know. Our whiskers know, our teeth know.

We know! the brother chimes.

The sister offers their tags: Mr Fluffy Man and Her Majesty The Queen.

Tybalt looks away—he's always scoffed at lengthy tags, as

if a cumbersome name could literally weigh down a cat by the neck—but I find that my sympathy for these two simply increases.

You are familiar with the threat that comes, I say.

Her Majesty The Queen tosses her head, affronted. That's what we said, right?

We'll be let out of the house this weekend! says Mr Fluffy Man.

Tybalt and I exchange glances: the weekend is three days away, too late.

This is our third house in six months, says Her Majesty The Queen. We have seen more neighbourhoods and full moons than you. We have stared down the throat of evil—of *evils*, for there is no single form, no limit to their invention in shapeshifting and corrupted familiarity.

The last one was like a lawnmower with leafblower arms! says Mr Fluffy Man.

Even my children are brave and wise to the threat, declares Her Majesty The Queen.

I do my best to remain expressionless, but Tybalt casts a doubtful glance at Her Majesty The Queen, her scrawny frame and relative youth, and Her Majesty The Queen catches it. She snarls.

You pampered glossy cats will never know! You might as well have been born tagged, dribbling into the world already soft and docile from humans' fawning hands. My brother and I, we were born wild! You would cry at the things we've seen—run snivelling to your humans without so much as a *here kitty-kitty.*

I killed a bird once! says Mr Fluffy Man.

Tybalt wanders away, tries again to rub against one of the spiny plants, and I permit myself an impatient tail-thump— Philip Glass, and now Tybalt, leaving me the tedious work of placating, pleasing. I try to meet Her Majesty The Queen with a resolute gaze. I have never borne children, it's true, I tell her. But there used to be one among us—Boots—

Boots, Her Majesty The Queen huffs, as if she's never heard a more ridiculous tag. I falter. Tybalt swivels his ear towards us.

What happened to Boots? asks Mr Fluffy Man.

For one merciful moment I see her face again, even smell her—blood on her breath, spit-shined coat.

She was our best, I say. And then the whitecoats killed her.

Her Majesty The Queen says, Ah, yes. I know her kind.

No you don't, I reply instantly, sprung like a mouse trap. I broaden my stance, as if meaning to set myself between Her Majesty The Queen and Boots's ghost.

What is the point of being only a fighter? To be only teeth? To be a collection of claws that cannot retract? Her Majesty The Queen sniffs. Your friend *Boots* was a failure at adaptation. Unequipped for survival.

I thought you said you were born wild, I say. Are you not a pampered glossy cat now, with your mice on a string? Your meat long dead, cubed, slid out of a foil sleeve?

Her Majesty The Queen yawns. A cat must know. A cat must taste the air. Smell the shape of the world, the walls. A cat must discern how to tame the human. How to use the human as a claw, a bell. When to fold, fall limp, perform deference. When to make marks. When to disappear. Don't take your swipes at me if your precious Boots did not grasp these truths.

And I suppose *you* know? Tybalt sighs. *This* cat must know if a cat *really* knows.

Her Majesty The Queen glowers. She flashes teeth. Mr Fluffy Man has one of those maws that looks like the curly part of an alto clef turned on its side. Agreeable in perpetuity.

Tybalt glances at me: he has thrown me the strategy. If you know what a cat must know, I announce, then *prove it*. Tame your human. Get them to let you leave the house before the weekend. Join us when the moon is full. Show us what you *know*.

In the daytime I dream of being inside a box, tilting and unsteady, a box inside which a cat must always kneel—crouch—make herself small.

And in this dream my box is not the only box: there are hundreds, carried over the sea—the large creaking boxes of the old ones, the first ones, the ones without tags—snatching rats and crunching them up all soft and wet and red. Tilting, heaving boxes, crawling with game, ripe with piss and spit and damp squirming lives.

And in this dream Boots claws her way free of the grave, throws the earth and bells from her body; she makes herself large. A yawn that turns into a growl that turns into a full-gutted waul.

And in this dream the moon swells like an eye, the whole neighbourhood bewitched by light. Bright water floods the piano room; our lady sinks into the murk.

And in this dream the whitecoats scoop me from my box—I am just a parcel of limbs to them, soft like a rat, a collared sack of muscle.

They inject me with darkness.

They scrape my womb from my body.

On the night of the full moon, we evade the human's plaintive last calls, we dissolve through doors and windows, we fold ourselves into secret holes. We require only the slimmest openings, the scantest moments of inattention—and our bells, out of respect for our mission, remain silent. Boots used to go the whole day without eating—it was the only way for her—lancing for the open door when the children left for school. Philip Glass and I linger longer than most, snuggled on the bed either side of our lady's knees, waiting for her last sigh of wakefulness, the minute sinking of her body underneath us. All day we have been close to her, weighing down her lap whenever she took a seat: not only did this make her reluctant to move, but also prone to forgetting to lock the flap. We let it close softly behind us.

There are cats gathering at the leisure centre, sparking white through the streetlights; already our nostrils burn from chlorine, an odour that grows into the shimmering outline of this neighbourhood, a gossamer noose. We ghost through the slots between fenceposts.

The swimming pool: sickly luminous, humming green and yellow, the lane markers quivering caterpillar-like. Among the assemblage of fangs and claws I seek out my familiar allies— there is Dumpling, using a palm tree as a scratching post; there is Kupo, studiously huddled. Tybalt has a quiet position near the waterslide. I can't see where Philip Glass has gone. The new ones, Mr Fluffy Man and Her Majesty The Queen, have just arrived; they catch sight of me, and Her Majesty The Queen narrows one eye in acknowledgement.

A murmur begins to take hold, bristling low in our throats, a collective shiver growing. If we could, we would throw off our collars—throw down our bells, our given names—and perhaps this is what the murmur is, a sound unhearable and untranslatable, a reclamation of what it is to be feline, to be cat, to be fur and tongue and teeth. The swimming pool's glow is brightening, morphing, everting; a hiss lurches from the depths, and the smell of chlorine is strong enough to manifest as surely as the walls of a box, as the dirt pressing down on Boots's wasting body.

There's a trembling underfoot, a prelude of vibrations issuing forth from the glowing pool, that swirling water, the lane dividers twisting. A terrible groan that climbs our spines, our teeth; the baubles on our collars quiver. We watch the water's impatient surface. The vibrations seem to coalesce, to unify into a regular beat, and somehow this quiet and militant pulse is more menacing than the arrhythmic trembling that preceded it.

Tick-tick-tick-tick-tick-tick-tick-tick-tick-tick-tick-tick-tick-tick

It rises—a wet snarl of hoses and flared gills, a dripping, fluttering maw. It flattens the night with a moan and our instinct is to cower, to make ourselves smaller, to lose ourselves in the drone of its evil—but then with a fearless waul Philip Glass leaps from nowhere and collides with the creature's throat, grappling for its webbed resin head, paying no heed to the churning water. This first strike gives us courage—our feeble murmurs transform into a frenzy of cries and spits and howls, and more and more cats lunge into the fray, disappearing into the chemical froth.

Those of us that remain on the side of the pool hiss and snap and thrash our tails; we swipe and dodge the water that slaps the pavement. We hurl strength to our brothers and sisters, we hurl every sound we've got from deep in our lungs. We take up the humans' nonsense chant:

YES.

YES.

YES YOU ARE.

YES YOU ARE.

Yes we are! And with that ringing thought I throw my legs forward, I clamp my ears against my skull, I take that flying leap into the water, I plunge into a soundless world. But is there ever such a thing, as long as a cat is alive? For even here in this foul chlorine pit there is a sound like a pedalled note dying in the hull of a piano, the indrawn breath of a choir, the first chord of the opera of my tag, and still that *tick-tick-tick* like a submarine timekeeper. I break the surface just as the creature arches a tubular limb out of the pool and slams it down. Cats sprawl, sloshed underwater or spat out onto the bricks, soaked bodies scrambling, but I latch my claws into the creature's limb and haul myself up. I tear at the ribbed hose, taste the deadness of human-made industry, like the whitecoats' gloves; I bite and scratch with a kitten's wildness. The cats on the pavement are still chanting, hissing, agitating fur, and finally the limb splinters open and I topple back into the water.

Somersaulting through the murk. There's a white wriggling shape below me that could be young Kupo—it's impossible to tell in this mono-scented place—so I drive myself downward underneath the body and buck us both up to the surface. We've barely scooped a breath before we must kick clear of the creature's smashing limbs, a new bruising wave— the feverish chanting thins as more cats pitch themselves into the fight. The pavement is littered with crumpled wet bodies heaving for air. There's a scurry of fur, a renewed cry: Tybalt climbs the creature, swinging for greater holds; his claws remain firm no matter how violently the creature tosses. Mr Fluffy Man is also climbing, keeping pace with Tybalt, snarling with a ferocity I could never have imagined coming from him. I clamber onto the bricks, spit out chlorine and thick saliva. My soggy fur presses me down like whitecoats' hands. My ribs are ready to buckle.

And then, a cold wet nudge beside me—Sister, says Her Majesty The Queen. I meet her prickly green eyes, her calm biscuit breath. She isn't Boots—no one will ever replace Boots—and yet in this moment she seems to offer herself not as an ally but a friend, another one tagged and wombless, another who knows. She nudges me again, a clumsy show of sympathy, and I feel for the first time the full depth of my mourning.

Come on, now, she says. For Boots.

For Boots, I reply.

We take the running leap together—straight for the creature's moonlit maw.

The next day will pass like an underwater dream, as if we are all of us still pedalling soundlessly in the yellow light. Only glorious flashes remain—the creature felled like a hatstand with the rug pulled out from underneath it, the crack of its broken limbs hitting the water, the pathetic fizz of bubbles as it sank back into its gloomy hole. And the shiver of triumph, the yowls of victory, the deep satisfying ache in our muscles.

Our humans fret over our wounds, at our coats rendered coarse from the chlorine—and we can only blink.

The streets are always quiet in the day following a full moon. Even Philip Glass is listless, bundling himself underneath the lady's bed, breathing dust and shadow. There will be no patrol today, no watchful eyes gleaming from the underbrush, no overturned earth.

Sooner than we think, it will be time to gather again. Maybe Her Majesty The Queen and Mr Fluffy Man will join us from now on, in Dumpling's yard, and nestle beside us like adjacent universes.

For now, though, I sink into the shapeless day, confident that the night will come, that the moon will wane, that there will be stars glistening like litter box crystals.

'You're a good girl, aren't you, O Fortuna?' our lady says from the other side of a dream. 'Who's a good girl?'

Our lady's warm hand, her hypnotic strokes, ushering me softly back to sleep.

WOULD YOU RATHER

What did it look like? A flaw in the morning, a hanging pixel. An iridescent chip in the shape of a rhombus, shimmering in the sky. Unnoticed for days, until all the bicycles lifted up on one wheel, and then the other; turned counter-clockwise in the air, handlebars raised like the antlers of a stag, sliding riders from their seats; floated towards the hole, and then through the hole, and then ...

And then? All the cushions—but only the square-shaped ones—tumbling skyward like Scrabble tiles returning themselves to the bag. And then? All the guinea pigs, their hind legs cycling furiously, dragged out from every hutch and pet store and burrow. That time—oh—the noise was unbearable, the screams of the poor things, the futile scrambling of their claws, succumbing to the hole just like the cushions and the bicycles. Then went the cheese-and-chives flavoured potato crisps, then Bratz dolls. Then lamingtons. Then beanies with pompoms.

They like to say that the child responsible was one Jennifer Green, but, if we were to be accurate, it was really a combination of Jennifer Green and her little sister, Freya Green. They had a little game going. Jennifer would ask Freya, 'Would you rather have a bicycle or rollerskates? Would you rather have a rabbit or a guinea pig? Would you rather have a Barbie or a Bratz doll?' And how exactly was Freya to know that she was answering for the whole world?

The world was faced with a rather terrible would-you-rather: would you rather be responsible for the murder of two little girls, or concede to the possibility of permanently and irreplaceably losing a very specific type of thing, any day, any time?

And there were still more terrifying possibilities that no one dared voice. Such as: what if one day Jennifer decided to ask, 'Would you rather be a firefighter or a zookeeper?' Or, 'Would you rather listen to The Wiggles or Hi-5?'

On the eve before the 'What To Do About The Green Sisters' referendum result was going to be announced, Benjamin Green sat down with his daughters. He had to sit on a beanbag, because, the day before, Jennifer had asked Freya, 'Would you rather sit on chairs or beanbags?', which sent their publicity officer into a spiral of worry about how this ill-timed would-you-rather would affect the swing voters. Benjamin sank into his beanbag and closed his eyes. He tried very hard not to hear those guinea pig screams, which still reverberated through his memory. He liked to imagine that, wherever they are now, the guinea pigs are actually happier, that perhaps his daughters are actually saving the world, one category of thing at a time, spiriting the world away to a kinder realm.

Benjamin sunk further into his beanbag while Jennifer and Freya set up teacups and saucers and positioned their stuffed toys around their tiny playtable. 'Daddy, sit closer,' Jennifer said, so Benjamin opened his eyes and wriggled his beanbag up to the edge of the playtable.

'Last tea party before bed, girls,' Benjamin said.

'It's not a tea party,' Jennifer said. 'It's supper.'

Benjamin anchored a smile. 'That's good, then.'

'We need to say grace first,' Jennifer said.

'Hold my hand, Daddy,' Freya said.

'It's just grace, Daddy,' Jennifer said. 'Don't worry. We'll say it. Just like Mummy used to.'

What did it look like? A hole in the memory of the sky, a tongue stumbling over a forgotten word. A pencil tethered to a cardboard booth, hovering over two checkboxes—twin portals, humming with loss. Daughter, daughter, father: eyes closed, heads bowed in prayer. Hands joined, as if to come before the Lord as a single category of thing—that must, as one, either float to the sky or hold to the earth.

EXCISION IN F-SHARP MINOR

Nora loosened her undies past her calves until they slipped to her ankles. She kicked them to the side of the ceramic pot. She placed one foot either side of the *Sempervivum arachnoideum* and hitched up her skirt. It took some adjusting to get the pressure just right so that the pee didn't list sideways and splash her thighs. Droplets clung to the cobweb filaments of the succulent. The nested leaves of the rosette guided the flow inexorably centreward. Nora watched the clouds in the sky.

♦

The night before that, Heidi said: 'I don't think you should be around the kids anymore.'

Aaron had finally stopped crying and was either asleep or pretending. Megan was practising her violin with her bedroom door closed.

Nora was holding the broken halves of the punch bowl that Dave had swept off the counter when he'd discovered what she'd done. Heidi, balancing ballerina-like on the coffee table, strained to reach the last dangling knot of the half-collapsed *Happy 9th Birthday!* foil banner.

'You don't want me around your kids anymore,' Nora repeated flatly. Heidi finally succeeded in pulling the string, and the banner flopped to the floor. 'That's going to be hard, because I live here. Unless you want me to move out.'

Heidi folded the banner, making sure that the segments were even and aligned, as if the accomplishment of this task was more important than re-boxing the uneaten birthday cake, or clearing the unclaimed goody bags lined up on the hall table, or looking Nora in the eye.

'Did you hear me, Heidi? I live here. How can I not be around the kids if I live here? Is Dave making you say this? Does Dave want me to move out? Is it Dave?'

Heidi said nothing. The only sound in the house was Megan squeaking at the top of an F-sharp minor scale.

♦

An hour before that, while the kids played musical chairs and Heidi and Dave fetched the birthday cake from the kitchen, Nora said, 'Hey guys! Who wants to hear the saddest song in the world?'

🐱

The night before that, Heidi and Nora packed the goody bags with snake lollies, Freddo Frogs, brittle Red Dot knick-knacks. 'Why isn't Dave helping us?' Nora asked.

Heidi sighed. 'Please don't.'

'No, really. Shouldn't you be asking these questions? How do you know the excision procedure really worked?'

Heidi sighed again. She snatched up a goody bag and dropped it with the finished ones.

'At the very least, it's good data, right?'

'Don't talk to me about data,' Heidi snapped. She rubbed her eyes. 'And promise me you'll stop experimenting on people outside the lab. Please. It's enough.'

🐱

The day before that, Nora looked on through the one-way glass into the testing chamber. The volunteers from the army reserves sat crumpled around the table, sobbing, while the song played for the fourth time. She was startled by an epiphany.

'We've only been testing it on adults,' she whispered.

🐱

The day before that, Dave brought home the *Sempervivum arachnoideum*. He'd even tied a bow around the ceramic pot.

Nora sat with Megan and Aaron in the living room while Dave and Heidi talked in the courtyard. 'Does this mean Dad can come to my birthday party?' Aaron asked.

'Maybe, kid,' Nora said. 'We'll have to see what your mum says.'

Megan frowned. 'Why did he bring her a cactus?'

'Well, you're probably too young to remember. But your mum loves succulents. She used to have heaps of them, right there in the courtyard. They're tough plants; they don't need much water. But, when your mum had that residency in Canada, your dad still managed to kill every single one of them.'

'Dad killed them?' Megan asked. 'On *purpose*?'

Nora winced. 'No. Forget I said that.'

'Come *on*, Aunt Nora,' Megan said. Eleven years old, and she'd already cultivated quite a good *bitch, please* look.

'Well. Promise you won't tell your mum I said this.'

'I promise.'

'She'll accuse me of treating you like mini adults instead of children.'

'I *promise*,' Megan said, and nudged her brother.

'Promise,' Aaron echoed.

'Well, I think your dad resented being left at home while your mum went away for a month. This was after Qantas folded, before your dad started up at Virgin. Even though money was tight, the opportunity to take up the residency was just too good for your mum to pass up. So, off she went, and your dad stayed to look after you lot. This was tricky for him. It's not that he couldn't do stuff—the laundry, making your school lunches, all that—but, I don't know, he just acted like it was all beneath him. Your mum would call him every day to chat, and he was still *but-but-but*-ing as if she wasn't oceans away. "But Megan likes it better when you make her sandwiches." "But Aaron says that I didn't wash his jumper the right way." So, yeah—I reckon he let the succulents die on purpose. Retaliation.'

Nora let her next breath hover painfully in her throat. Aaron turned his furrowed gaze away from her, but Megan looked sharp and thoughtful, like she was doing mental math and Nora had just given her the numbers to make things add up. 'It's an excision, isn't it?' Megan said. 'Like with you and your sadness and that song?'

Nora nodded.

'But then, what's in it?'

'I couldn't supervise your dad's procedure, you understand—conflict of interest—but my guess? *That* little beauty'— Nora gestured to the glass doors overlooking the courtyard, where Heidi and Dave were hugging, the succulent nestled snugly in its ceramic pot on the ground between them—'that right there is your daddy's fragile masculinity.'

A week before that, Heidi shouted, 'Fuck you, Nora!' and stormed out of the living room, her face soaked in tears.

'I'm sorry!' Nora called after her. 'I'm sorry I ambushed you!' The song was still playing on her laptop. 'I just wanted to see how you'd react without forewarning,' she said quietly.

The day before that, the head musicologist stepped out of the testing chamber, spectacles in hand, dabbing his eyes with his shirt cuff. His spine seemed crushed as he stood before Nora and the other scientists. He clutched a clipboard under his arm.

'Here's what we observed,' the musicologist said. His hands trembled as he replaced his spectacles and lifted the clipboard.

'The song is in F-sharp minor, 6/4 time, and advances at a tempo of approximately thirty-three dotted minim beats to the minute.

'The instrument is indeterminate. Something like a celesta, but also like a flute. We would describe the timbre as somehow both bright and muffled.

'The song has a contrapuntal texture and appears to be produced entirely by the one instrument.

'We would characterise the song as adhering to a binary structure, with no repeated motifs or themes.'

The musicologist lowered the clipboard. 'I must apologise for the elementary nature of our observations. It was very difficult. We were affected almost instantly.'

Nora liked the way the musicologist's voice frayed a little on the 'instantly'. She *didn't* like how she couldn't nod like the other scientists, smile with tender empathy like the other scientists. They'd turned off the sound to the observation room so that they could study the musicologists without being affected by the song themselves, but Nora wished she could have listened to it again. It was hers, after all. Her heart wanted to hear it.

The week before that, Nora snapped her laptop shut. Heidi wiped away tears with her knuckle. She rubbed her other hand over her chest in circles, as if trying to collect her scattered heartbeats. 'Why couldn't I stop crying?'

'It's the same for everyone we test. You should have seen the naval officers we had in the lab the other day. All of them—bawling.'

'But *you* weren't crying.'

'Right. I guess because, you know. It's *my* grief.'

'So if I were to, say, transpose the song to a different key, would it still have the same effect? Or if I were to play the melody on a cello, or a piano, or a flute?'

'No. It's just the original song.'

'Has anything like this happened with other excisions?'

'No—but as far as we know, this is the first time the

excision has taken the form of a song. Most people pick an object, like a medicine ball, or a wax figurine of a dolphin, or a tennis shoe.'

'Do you think if someone brought in a blank book—say, they decided to excise their anxiety into this book—would words appear on the pages? And would reading the book, I don't know, make the reader break out into a sweat, or give them heart palpitations?'

'Well, my colleagues are reluctant to test it out. They don't want to create more problems, like with the song.'

'You'd have to create another example, surely,' Heidi said, 'in order to study the phenomenon properly.'

Nora grinned. 'Now you're thinking like a scientist.'

Heidi smiled bleakly. She reached for a tissue. 'Well, I needed a good cry. Dave won't stop messaging me.'

'Why haven't you blocked him?'

Heidi's eyes sharpened. 'Don't start.'

'Hey. This has nothing to do with my general loathing for Dave. He's bothering you, so you should block him.'

'He's Megan and Aaron's father! I can't *block* him. If *you* had a family of your own—' Heidi faltered. Her cheeks turned pink with shame.

'Don't worry.' Nora patted the laptop. 'My grief's all gone now.'

The day before that, Nora said to her therapist, 'It's not like I don't get sad anymore. I still do, sometimes. But it's so much easier to carry now. At least I can get through the day, you know? I can get out of bed. I can take a shower. I can pull on my clothes. I can make breakfast. I can *eat* breakfast. I can go to work.'

'It sounds like the excision procedure was a positive step for you, Nora. I know you had your doubts. You said it felt like a betrayal.'

'I did. But it doesn't feel like a betrayal anymore. My pain is no longer the centre. It used to be the thing I had instead of Gwen, but now I feel like I can have a relationship with her— with the memory of her—that isn't defined by the loss of her.'

'That sounds like an improvement.'

'It's like all the stuff that you and I have talked about that has never actually made sense to me—stuff that seemed kind of like bullshit, no offence—mindfulness and staying present and watching your thoughts go by like clouds—all of that can be true now.'

'You're *present*.' The therapist smiled. 'And how's your living situation at the moment? Are you still staying with your sister?'

'Yeah. I hope I can stay with her for a bit longer. I saw Dave in the waiting room at work the other day.'

'Oh? That's interesting.'

'Yeah. I think he's going to try to win Heidi back somehow.'

The therapist nodded again. 'Perhaps this is another thing you might like to consider excising. I don't mean that literally, of course. But I think you could try to let go of this need to protect Heidi from her decisions about Dave. Of course you can't help but notice things you don't like about him. But you don't have to take action.' The therapist let the fingers of her fist unfurl like dandelion spores. 'They're just thoughts in the sky.'

A week before that, Nora asked, 'Would I be allowed on the research team?'

The head of department looked at his solicitor, who issued a tight nod.

Nora shrugged and said, 'Sure.'

She signed her named on the dotted line.

An hour before that, Nora checked herself in for her post-excision appointment. She arrived in the consultation room to find a cluster of her colleagues at the desk. 'What's going on?' she asked.

They were staring at a clear plastic envelope with a yellow stick-on label with her case number written on it. Inside the envelope was a CD-ROM.

'There's something strange about your excision,' someone finally said.

The day before that, Nora lay inside the tunnel of the EXC-1510. It was like being inside a pristine seashell designed by Apple.

'Are you comfortable, Nora?'

'Yes.'

'I suppose it might feel a little weird to you, being the one inside the machine.'

'Yes. I suppose it does.'

'I understand you've brought in a blank CD-ROM.'

'Yes.'

'I haven't seen one of these in ages.'

'It's Gwen's. She had stacks of them.'

'I see.'

The rhythmic clack of a keyboard.

'I just didn't know what else to bring.'

'It's okay, Nora. You don't have to justify yourself. The CD will be fine.'

Clack. Clack.

'Well. There's no need for me to go through the preamble, is there, Nora?'

'No.'

'I'll skip ahead to the legal stuff.'

'Sure.'

'You confirm that you understand that this is an experimental procedure, and that the permanence and efficacy of the excision procedure are still under study.'

'Yes.'

'You confirm that your excision adviser has explained the risks and benefits of the procedure at a prior consultation.'

'Yes.'

'You understand that once the excision process is underway, you will not be able to withdraw your consent.'

'Yes.'

'Good. Thank you, Nora.'

The clacks of the keyboard became livelier. A vivacious hum emanated from the machine.

'This is the part where you tell me about Gwen. How about you tell me the story of the first time you met her?'

'It was ...' Nora struggled. 'It was ...'

'Nora, there are tissues in the compartment to your left if you need them.'

'Thank you.' Nora took a tissue and blew her nose. She didn't know what to do with the tissue after that, so she just balled it up in her fist.

'Tell me about the first time you met Gwen.'

'It was ... at a party with Heidi's Conservatorium friends. I didn't know anybody. I hated Heidi for dragging me along. We played that drinking game—I Never. Someone said, "I never pissed in an enemy's pot plant." Everyone laughed except me. It was obvious it was engineered for just one person. Only one girl drank. It was Gwen.'

'What a way for her to make an entrance into your life.'

'I know. I thought: I wish I could be that fearless. I wish I could give zero fucks. I wish I could make out with that girl.'

'I'm so sorry she's gone.'

'Thank you.'

The machine beeped. 'Nora, we're ready for the excision. Shall we proceed?'

Nora closed her eyes—felt, for the last time, the void in her chest which dragged her inexorably centreward. 'Yes.'

HAPPY SMILING UNDERWEAR GIRLS PARTY

Ha ha ha ha ha ha ha! We're having the BEST conversation right now about Amber's mint-striped boyleg briefs, which are really comfortable to dance in, she says, doing a little butt wriggle, and we laugh some more because it really *is* amazing to dance in these briefs and nobody has had a wedgie since the party started and it's almost noon. I'm wearing hipster bikini briefs with grey and white stripes and a black T-shirt bra with lace detail and I am having so much fun at this party even though I am not wearing very festive colours. I am certainly not wearing Jessica's zebra print hipster string bikini and fuchsia bandeau bra! But this is still a fun party. Hang on, it's the moment in the party where we all stand in a chaotic can-can line with our arms around each other and make long lean Xs with our legs and laugh because we are all best friends that wear different underwear styles and we love hanging out together in our diverse underwears.

Now Verity wants to have a pillow fight so we all grab a white pillow and start smacking each other and dodging and laughing until our hair is all messed up. Verity's plunge bra is white and has a big blue glittered *O* on her right cup and *MG* on her left cup and when I asked her before what she thought of it she said that she feels like her boobs are always in a state of breathless excitement, which is a reflection of her extroverted character, and she is really happy to be an unmarried 18–25-year-old low-to-middle-income earner with an active lifestyle and two or more pets.

And we're all really happy because none of us is on our period right now because we're all really good friends and our periods are synced. Everyone is relieved about this because they don't want to be like Hayley who *did* have her period today and couldn't come to the party. She might get kicked out of our group if she misses another party but that's just my personal speculation because right now we're simply having too much fun to gossip about disorganised klutzy Hayley itching in her blood-soaked Ultrathin.

Ha ha ha ha ha ha ha! Verity's the successful outgoing one and Jessica's the sexy Good Kind Of Slut and Amber's the Girl Next Door and I'm the Asian one, or perhaps more accurately the Diverse one, because no matter who you are you need to wear underwear and I represent a demographic that wields modest-to-considerable Buying Power and my Non-Threatening Otherness makes me One Of The Girls and I am so so grateful to be One Of The Girls so I wear my not-as-festive underwear obediently and laugh at Verity's jokes.

Jessica insists that we do a magazine quiz called What Kind Of Cupcake Are You and I know without looking that I am Vanilla. Jessica reads out each question to Amber and traces the flowchart with her glitter-varnished fingernail and I notice that Jessica has recently added a new charm to her bracelet, a small silver chubby loveheart with the initials KH engraved on it, and I ask who KH is.

Jessica falls silent. There's a chill in the room that wasn't there before, as if one of us has done something unthinkable, like taken a shit or something, and Jessica hitches up her bandeau bra which has become lopsided in this long terrible moment. And then, Jessica smiles and says, Wouldn't *you* like to know, and winks saucily, and we all laugh and everything is okay again, and Amber is a Red Velvet Cupcake, and Verity initiates a new round of pillowfighting and we are all grateful, we are so fucking grateful.

Later over kale and ginger mocktails Amber tells me the difference between a balconette bra and a push-up bra, which is fascinating, and Verity sighs and says she cannot wait to find her One True Bra, because even though we all love the bras that we are wearing there is a super strong understanding amongst all people with breasts that somewhere out there is a bra so comfortable, so moulded to the shape of one's body, that it's like wearing nothing at all, and as long as we keep browsing and buying bras we will all eventually find our One True Bra. Jessica insists that we do a magazine quiz called What Kind Of Salad Dressing Are You and I know without looking that I'm Vinaigrette.

I notice Jessica's KH loveheart again and it nags me like a twisted bra strap but I will not mention the KH loveheart again. Instead I turn to Verity and ask to see the latest photos of her Pom Terrier and soon we're all cooing over a phone slideshow of the perky little thing. Some of the photographs contain Verity herself dressed in a navy blue polka-dot halter-neck bikini as she cuddles the dog while reclining in a sun chair and I wonder: who took the photographs? Because they can't all possibly be selfies. Verity snaps her phone case shut before I can scrutinise the photographs too closely and announces that it's time to eat. She passes around a platter piled high with glistening strawberries with their leaves still on and we each place a strawberry in our mouths and hold it there between our puckered lips like it's not sexual or anything. Ha ha ha ha ha ha ha ha! I don't even know the name of Verity's dog.

Jessica insists we do a magazine quiz called What Does Your Vaginal Discharge Say About You and I know without looking that mine says You're A Shy Bland Virgin; How's 'Waiting For The Right One' Been Working Out For You? Verity hotly denies that she even produces observable vaginal discharge and Amber says that she uses Libra pantyliners to keep her underwear fresh and Verity has a look in her eye like she's taking mental notes.

On the page after the Vaginal Discharge quiz is an interview with Kit Harington from *Game of Thrones* and we all sigh and wish we could be Rose-Leslie-as-Kit-Harington's-On-Screen-Love-Interest and Rose-Leslie-As-Kit-Harington's-Real-Life-Sweetheart. On the opposite page to the interview is a tear-out black-and-white poster of Kit Harington's tousled curls and Kit Harington's soulful chocolate stare and Kit Harington's white button-down shirt that foretells the hard muscular terrain of Kit Harington's abs. And as I am falling into the smiling shadows beneath Kit Harington's eyes I realise that Kit Harington's initials are KH.

I stop falling and I bite my lip because I know I can't say anything, I just can't say anything. I will not survive if I say anything. I will not ever be allowed at another underwear party again. So I stare at Kit Harington, overcome by desire, aching with the certainty that Kit Harington would never love me because when I did the What Kind Of Man Could Possibly Want You quiz I got Steady Bookish Nice Guy and Kit Harington seems more like a Brooding Overthinker Dedicated To His Craft.

But then I notice Amber's eye drawn to the interview, and the abbreviation 'KH' for each of Kit Harington's answers. Jessica, she exclaims. Do you love Kit Harington?

At first Jessica deflects—Of course, we all love him!—but

then Amber takes Jessica's wrist in her hand and overturns the silver loveheart so that the KH is exposed.

No, you *really* love him, Amber says.

Jessica sits there frozen and uncomfortable as if one of us has done something unthinkable, like farted or something, and Jessica withdraws her wrist from Amber's grasp, and I know then absolutely that Jessica doesn't actually know what KH stands for, just like Verity's dog doesn't have a name, and the whole afternoon begins to crumble.

And I am spurred by determination that I can hardly understand—to save Jessica, to save all of us.

So I announce:

I know. I know what KH stands for.

And for the first time ever all of my friends are looking at me. I have their attention. My face turns pink and I flounder and I can feel the seat of my briefs creeping up perilously close to my ass crack.

I blurt out: It stands for Kitty Hellcat, which is Jessica's secret crimefighting alter-ego.

Everyone is silent. The party teeters, knife-edged. Jessica is staring at me.

And slowly, she smirks.

How did you know I was Kitty Hellcat? Jessica asks.

And I say, Because I'm a witch.

And a thrilling regal warmth unrolls through my body and I draw myself up to my full height and I say it again.

I. AM. A. WITCH.

Jessica springs to her feet and says, I want to join you!

Jessica and I stand on the bed high above everybody else and shriek with laughter and Amber shouts I Am The Queen Of All The Spiders and Verity shouts I Am A Malevolent Self-Learning Operating System. Jessica and I help them climb up on the bed and we are so tall we can grow through the ceiling and so high our lungs are filled with legends and ghosts and songs of our bravery. We jump off the bed. We tip the contents of Amber's pencilcase onto the floor and pop the lids off Sharpies and draw on our arms and each other's arms and on the walls with big-fisted letters and slashes and curse words. We are overtaken by some mad urge to *make*, to create, to mindfuck, and we strip the sheets from the bed and soon the room is festooned with doona shreds, and Jessica has fashioned a bitchin' cape for herself, and I snap the slats from the base of the bed and create ragged effigies of every girl here. Amber grabs handful after handful of strawberries and shoves them in her mouth and smears the red fruit all over her body and we all join in until juice runs down our necks and into our bras and cleavage.

We set upon the poster of Kit Harington and divide him between us. Each girl may do with Kit Harington as they wish. Verity makes a little origami chatterbox and Amber screws him up into little paper balls and swallows them and Jessica rearranges the letters of his name into HANG KNIT RIOT and I paste his eyes onto an effigy and then set fire to it with a lighter that Verity confesses she always smuggles into our parties. Then we decide that we shouldn't be so hard on poor Kit Harington so we put the fire out and each give the scorched effigy a kiss and tuck him in to what is left of the bed.

And we all agree that this is the best party we've ever had and Amber hacks up a slimy ball of Kit Harington. Ha ha ha ha ha ha! Jessica sighs and says that we're her best friends, and it's so nice to have best friends, and she is right. We huddle together like bunnies in a nest of doona shreds until we fall asleep.

DISOBEYING

Harper Wen-Fox is too old to be embarrassed. She has weathered the lonely signing table before. It doesn't matter that Jackson Holloway's queue stretches all the way out of the signing tent. So long, that Jackson's Post-it Note–wielding publicist now weaves her way to each cluster of waiting fans—powdery middle-aged suburban book club types and Doc Martened, plaid-shirted types—chirping, 'Hello! Who is Jack signing for today? How do you spell that? Thank you!' and slipping *Blue Swims Bridge* from their eager grip, opening to the title page, and smoothing the Post-it Note there with a confident thumb. *Every time*, Harper admires. *No fumbling. She opens it bang-on the title page every time.*

Harper's session had been a bit of a disaster. The moderator, whose sweet red hairclips matched perfectly her red ballet flats, had perhaps committed to chairing more sessions than she could effectively rehearse for. She kept making a big deal out of not knowing how to pronounce things in Harper's novel. 'Now, the world of *A Balanced Ensemble* is loosely based on the, oh I'm sorry I'm going to mangle this, the Qing? Dynasty? And it centres on a group of assassins disguised as performers in a *xiqu* company, did I say that right? *Xiqu?*'

Eventually, as the moderator crawled through a wincing enunciation of the protagonist's name, Harper said: 'Just make an attempt and move on.' Harper heard a nervous laugh in the audience, and the moderator blushed as red as her ballet flats, and she did not look Harper in the eye again. Harper had tried to sound gentle, but perhaps she came off as too abrupt; perhaps the audience didn't like her much after that. The moderator was so young, after all, and so very white. Harper is neither of those things.

Harper doesn't wish the moderator ill. It's not like Harper herself could have done any better with the slack elastic of her thoroughly Australianised tongue. If Harper wishes anything, it's that she had a publicist who could tell her that she doesn't have to sit at this signing table any longer. She'd signed two copies of *A Balanced Ensemble*, but five copies of *The Ocean's Memoir*. 'It's nice that this is still floating around,' Harper said to the signees, not knowing what else to say. *Floating around*, like *The Ocean's Memoir* was persistent jetsam bobbing around the exquisite shipwreck of her life.

Harper hasn't read a single review of *A Balanced Ensemble*. She doesn't need to. She can imagine.

A puzzling stylistic departure for Wen-Fox, best known for the

Vogel Award-winning biography The Ocean's Memoir.

One would be forgiven for thinking that The Ocean's Memoir *and* A Balanced Ensemble *are authored by two completely different people; although, to be fair to Wen-Fox, eight years have elapsed between each title.*

For all its audacity and imagination, A Balanced Ensemble *will confuse—and likely, disappoint—fans of* The Ocean's Memoir, *but will it win new ones?*

The touchscreen of Harper's phone lights up. A text from Jude Fox: *Omg mom these are not audience questions they are audience life stories. How was your session, are you free yet?*

Jude had been nine-going-on-ten years old when Harper won the Vogel. *A decade old!* he liked to say. *Double digits!* Harper was on the cusp of a milestone age then, too: less than a month shy of slipping out of the eligible age range for the Vogel. Thirty-five years old. When one turns from 'a young writer' into … 'a writer'? Harper doesn't know.

That was also back when the *Fox* part of Harper's surname meant something. Sometimes, Harper thinks: if only Patrick had the decency to divorce her *before* her first book was published. But most of the time, she doesn't mind. The *Fox* makes her feel shrewd, cunning, quick-witted. She'd come away from her marriage with a dapper hyphenated surname, and Jude.

Harper swipes a reply to Jude: *It went fine. Meet you at the University Club?*

Jude stopped coming to Harper's writerly engagements

years ago—a fact she is ordinarily relieved about, though perhaps his presence might have been reassuring at today's session. They might have been able to meet eyes across the auditorium and smile. But, knowing her shit-stirrer of a son, Harper suspects he wouldn't have been able to resist trolling at question time. Crafting some contorted question that looped in *Xerxes* and *Don Quixote* and *creating positive qi* while maintaining gleeful aggressive eye contact with the moderator.

At least she'll be headed to the University Club soon, and they can debrief over hot chips.

She is slipping her phone into her handbag and wondering whether her writer's lanyard entitles her to a discount at the University Club when she first sees the stranger. He's walking past the still-burgeoning queue for Jackson Holloway— holding a book to his chest, title-side-in—towards Harper's space at the signing table. The colour of the book's jacket is just a few shades off pure black, neither the indigo of *The Ocean's Memoir* nor the orange of *A Balanced Ensemble*. Harper glances around, but the author to her left is pushing back her chair and slinging her tote bag over her shoulder, and to her right Jackson Holloway is opening *Blue Swims Bridge* to the Post-it-Note–marked page and looking up at his next reader with a warm smile and, at the far end of the signing table, three authors from a just-concluded session are taking their seats—but the stranger with the book is, absolutely definitely, headed for her.

Harper sinks back into her chair. What'll it be, she

thinks—*I'm trying to write a book myself and …? Can you tell me how you got published?*

'Hello,' says the stranger. 'Could you please sign my copy of your book?'

'Oh, I think—' *I think you're mistaken.* But the rest of her sentence falls away when the stranger places the book in front of her.

DISOBEYING

A Novel

BY

HARPER WEN-FOX

'I loved it,' the stranger says. 'It's become my favourite of your books.'

Harper is as firmly stuck-in-place as if smoothed there by Jackson Holloway's publicist's thumb. *This is not my book.*

'Oh,' she says. 'Oh. Thank you? I mean. Thank you.'

'I loved the ending especially,' the stranger says. 'It was a surprise, but it also just felt so right, you know? Like, of *course.*'

Harper looks up at the stranger's smiling face, and down at the book with her name on it. Up at the stranger's face again. Down.

Disobeying.

The stranger is waiting. The social contract compels Harper's tremoring hand forward to pick up what she has ascertained to be the least shitty of the signing table's pens.

Disobeying.

Could it be (no, come on) a *different* Harper Wen-Fox? She doesn't want to touch the book, as if it's a trap poised to spring, but she does. It's not a pristine book—the corners of the pages flicked-up, a little crease in the spine—but it has not been mistreated. She imagines this stranger holding the book open in one hand as he sways on the peak hour train to Perth; she imagines him in a leather armchair, placing his reading glasses in the fold and letting the pages collapse on top of them while he gets up to check his dinner in the oven.

Harper opens *Disobeying.* Before she can find the title page, she flips past the *About the Author* page: the biography, which is absolutely definitely about her (*Harper Wen-Fox is a Malaysian-born West Australian writer who won the 2013 Australian/Vogel's Literary Award*), and the accompanying headshot, which is the same one that appears in *The Ocean's Memoir* and *A Balanced Ensemble* (I should really get a new one taken, thinks Harper).

Harper sweeps to the title page. 'Um …' she looks up at the stranger.

'Daniel,' he says.

'Daniel,' she repeats in a stupor. She twists the cap off the pen. Writes: *Dear Daniel, Thank you for giving my book a home. Harper Wen-Fox.* The pen decides to withhold ink on the downstroke of the 'F' in *Fox*, so she has to do it again, darker. It's now that she wonders whether this is some kind of prank engineered by Patrick, or Jude.

'I'm sorry to have missed your session just now,' Daniel

says. 'I was at the "Deception and Authenticity" panel. It ran overtime, too. Always the way, isn't it? All the sessions you want to go to, overlapping.'

'I know exactly what you mean.'

'Are you in any other sessions?'

'No, actually, I'm done for the day. I'm about to go meet my son.'

And Harper thinks, *seriously?* This is what we're going to talk about? Generic literary festival banter?

Disobeying.

Harper closes the book and rests her hand on the jacket. The cover doesn't give away any clues: just that not-quite-black background and the title inside a not-quite-white circle. A thick, tall serif typeface. If it *is* a trick—from Patrick, or Jude—then it's a very handsome one.

'I'm sorry,' Harper says, staring at the book. Her mind rolls fibs that might explain why she's holding on to the book for so long. *I haven't seen this edition before. I'm just remembering my mother, who died right before this was published. Actually, this is not my book.* But Daniel doesn't seem to require an excuse. He just smiles his patient smile. His eyes are very blue and he is as combed and cleanfaced as a choirboy, but his smile is old, fatherly; his syllables creak like leather. He'll do this throughout their short conversation—hover in this ageless zone.

'How old's your son?' Daniel asks.

'Nearly eighteen now. Cute, and knows he is. Likes to pronounce and spell *mom* the American way. Likes to read my books and then not tell me what he thinks about them.'

'Was he the inspiration for Ritchie?'

'The inspiration for …?'

Daniel's eyes drop to *Disobeying* in her hand.

'Oh,' she scrambles. 'Ritchie.' The name sounds wrong in her mouth. 'Maybe a little bit? I suppose—how can he not be? He's so important to me. But I find that … I find that my characters, though they might start out being representative of someone I know … they grow into their own person, you know, and I can't claim them anymore.'

What she should have done before, Harper realises, instead of gawking at the *About the Author* page, was try to glimpse the imprint page, which would have told her the copyright year. But she can't very well open the book again. In any case, she can't decide what would have been more frightening to see: a copyright year in the past, or a copyright year in the future? Both seem distressingly possible, sitting here in front of Daniel, whose plain white crewneck and dusky jeans are devoid of era signifiers, which, she supposes, is in itself a signifier: he's like a time-traveller from *Looper*.

'I guess it would be a strange feeling for your son,' Daniel says, 'to see himself, or a part of himself, in your book.'

'Yes, I guess it would be.'

But *would* Jude really feel that way? Harper thinks: *oh no, he'd love it*. Love it like a cat being scratched under the chin. *Oh, I'm im-por-tant to you, am I?*

She can't help smiling exasperatedly and fondly, which

Daniel mistakes as being directed at him.

'I'm sorry—you probably want to be going.'

'Oh, no, not at all—thank you. Thank you for reading my book.' She slides *Disobeying* towards him even though what she really wants to do is gather this book in her hands and hold the pages to her face as if she could inhale the ink. She doesn't know how to keep Daniel talking, how to keep him and *Disobeying* here. Her desperation reminds her of the first time Patrick left, a resemblance that startles her into pushing *Disobeying* off the signing table completely.

'Oh!'

'No, no, that was my fault! Here, I'll get it!'

Daniel kneels to pick up the book. As he stands, he brushes the loose grass off the cover, like a father might neaten the fringe of his child. He meets Harper's eye and chuckles sheepishly.

'You know,' Daniel says, 'I remember exactly where I was when I read this.'

'You do?'

'I was in my brother's house in Sydney. My only brother. He'd just passed away, you see. Our parents—they've been gone for years now. My brother didn't marry. I was packing up his house. I was making funeral arrangements.'

Harper corrects her previous imaginings. She places Daniel and *Disobeying*, instead, in a picked-over house—Daniel, perhaps, wedged under a reading lamp propped up on a tower of cardboard boxes, surrounded by the walls' blockish ghosts of furniture and whitegoods that he'd managed to Gumtree away. 'That must have been difficult,' Harper says eventually.

'Your book was my friend,' Daniel says, in the kind of bluntly factual tone that reminds her of a young Jude. 'I really just wanted to tell you that. Thank you. Thank you for writing this book.'

She pulls up a smile. Nods. 'Thank you for coming up to talk to me. It was nice to meet you.'

'And you.'

And then he's walking away, *Disobeying* tucked in his hand, swinging slightly. The white pages between those not-quite-black covers flash like a rescue light fading over a dark horizon. Into another universe.

In the week that follows, Harper will half-heartedly revisit her theory that it was all a prank—she'll experiment with dropping the word *disobeying* into her conversations with Jude to see if he reacts. But it's a surprisingly difficult word to employ organically, and after a while Jude will say, 'Oh, is this a game? Are we saying ominous things to each other? Okay. Hey Mom, your *foreshadowing* looks nice today. How would you feel if I got some *foreshadowing* of my own? You know, sometimes I'm just so scared of my own *foreshadowing*. Jumping at *foreshadowing*.'

Various permutations of search terms, plugged into various

search engines, will only yield unhelpful questions. *Did you mean* Disobedience *by Naomi Alderman? Did you mean* The Ocean's Memoir *by Harper Wen-Fox?*

Harper will decide not to call Patrick about the incident, which probably turns out to be a good decision, because Patrick becomes engaged to his girlfriend the following autumn, and they marry in spring. When Jude returns from the reception, he will loyally report, 'Hideous. Maudlin. An overstuffed production. And the catering: woeful.' And as he unknots his bowtie and slinks to his bedroom: 'Dad said congratulations on the new book.'

A Balanced Ensemble will be remembered as *a modest success*; it will be just popular enough to earn a second print run, and it will be optioned for a stage adaptation that will never pan out.

There will be a little while when, on the way to work, Harper will constantly see Patrick beaming down at her from billboards in bright federal election colours. Sometimes he'll appear on the news with his second wife, Franka, and he'll be swinging Franka's two-year-old up to perch on his shoulders while the cameras flash approvingly. Jude will note that Franka doesn't take Patrick's surname. 'I guess the alliteration would be a bit weird,' Jude says. Patrick will fail to win the seat of Swan, and after that Harper won't see or hear of him again until he dies of a brain aneurysm shortly before Jude graduates university.

At the funeral, where she will be relieved that nobody

asks who she is, Harper will think: Patrick has left her three, four times before; how is it possible to feel anything about this final leaving besides the most generic sadness, the most wooden mourning? It's that child she saw on Patrick's shoulders whom she will feel sadness for—so many upheavals for a life so young. Jude will be sombre at the funeral; he will take his mother's hand in his, but will not cry.

Jude will stay with Harper throughout his twenties, will bring home this girlfriend and that boyfriend; sometimes, Harper might even hear them arguing—will hear, through his bedroom door, Jude's voice turn uncharacteristically high and pleading. It will seem to her to be a fifty-fifty split as to whether Jude is the dumper or the dumpee in these relationships. Jude will not move out until he meets Miguel, and even then the two of them will be at the house at least once a week. Miguel will be as soft and guileless as Jude is angular and contrarian—will be easily recruited to pruning the lemon tree and troubleshooting the wifi, and he will always tell Harper what he thinks about her books.

Harper will never write a book called *Disobeying*. But one night, after clambering through—and giving up on—a thickety dissertation chapter from one of her postgrad students, she will open a new document. Type, bold and centred, *Disobeying*, to see what it would look like.

And then be seized by the chill of error—an interdimensional lurch—like crunching into second gear when you meant to change to fourth. She will close the window without saving the document.

No, not *Disobeying*. She will publish two books after *A Balanced Ensemble*. The first, *The Art of Weaving Lace*, will be another *modest success*. She will be invited again to the same literary festival, but her session will be pleasant this time, dull even. She will linger at the signing table long after her queue is exhausted, waiting for Daniel to appear, but he won't. Instead, Harper's neighbour at the signing table will be that same young moderator with the sweet red hairclips and ballet flats, who will have just published her first book. Harper will be gracious enough to smile at her; together, they will admire the interminable signing queue of this year's Jackson Holloway (Byron Mitchell Hull, *The Season of Burning Foals*), laugh about the lonely awkwardness of their predicaments; the debut author will proudly show Harper her special signing pen, which has a Scottish Terrier on the lid. Such a small world—and yet, Harper never sees Daniel again.

Harper will not have to endure the lonely signing table for her last book. The day after approving the final typeset pages, she will be driving to a faculty meeting when her car will be T-boned by a four-wheel-drive running a red light, an incident completely lacking in poetry or any sense of dramatic irony. She will be extricated from her capsized car and bundled into an ambulance; Jude will receive the phone call from emergency services as he is lining up to purchase a sandwich.

There will be a somewhat aquatic quality to it all: the

churning of Harper's unconscious mind, the spill of memories and emergency lights and sirens twisting in the gloom. Pain as heavy as an ocean; she will have to go deeper, under and under, a desperate pearl diver that has no choice but to descend.

In Harper's one moment of true lucidity, she will peel open her eyes like reluctant mussels—will see, in that colourless hospital room, a sleepless Jude with uncombed hair and slumped shoulders, creased shirt sleeves folded up unevenly at the cuffs. She will say: 'Ritchie.'

And oh, the way his breath stops in his throat will be like a thumbtack pushed into her heart. He will press himself close to her side and clutch her hand. 'No, Mum, it's Jude.'

But it will be as if the darkness has sloughed off all the words that she knows, and she will only be able to say, 'Ritchie.' She will succumb to her injuries shortly after.

What was the last thing that Daniel said? He said that he remembered where he was when he first read *Disobeying*. From the bottom of her painful ocean, Harper will remember: she will remember where she was when she began her fourth and final book. It will not involve committing words to a page. It will happen when Jude and Miguel take her to a Korean barbeque restaurant as a belated fifty-third birthday present. It'll be one of those restaurants nestled within a dining precinct in a shopping centre courtyard, and after they are seated, Harper will ask Jude and Miguel, 'Do either of you know whether there's a restroom in here?'

'Oh, it won't be in here, Mom,' Jude will say. 'You'll have to go back out into the courtyard. There's a corridor.' He will hold out two fists knuckle-side-up, like a prelude to a child's guessing game. He'll bounce the left fist and then the right one. 'You'll see an Indian restaurant on this side, and then a Thai restaurant on this side. The corridor to the restrooms is in-between.'

And Harper will look at her son's extended fists and marvel at this little demonstration, these two precious fists. It's a mannerism that she knows he didn't get from her, nor from Patrick: it is something her son picked up himself, and made his own, and despite the smallness of the gesture, the nothing-ness of it, Jude will appear to Harper as someone entirely his own person, over whom she has no claim.

And a strange sort of love will unfurl itself: not a motherly love, but a writerly conviction that this particular moment cannot be faithfully replicated, that any description will fail, but an attempt must nonetheless be made.

Harper will thank Jude and leave him and Miguel behind. The shopping centre courtyard will be uncommonly lush and green as she makes her way through, smelling smoke and charred meat and spices, turning the previous moment over in her mind, and, although she will not know it then, she is shepherding a new thing into the universe.

THIS IS NOT A TREEHOUSE

There's something I've been meaning to ask you. What are you doing? I mean, I know what you're *doing*—you've been saying for ages that you want to build a treehouse. It's a dream you've had since you were a child. I know it's not fair to judge something when it's not yet complete. And I'm not trying to criticise you. But I am pretty sure that this is not a treehouse.

The neighbours will complain about this. They were nice about the incident when all of your bees drowned in their swimming pool. And they were very accommodating that time when you hosted Vuvuzelafest. But I think it might be a struggle not to mention *this*.

It is casting a significant shadow over their house.

If this is about last night, I am so sorry. I just really wanted to sneak up on you. I thought I'd bring it back, you know. Sneaking. It used to be one of our favourite activities. We would always be sneaking up on each other and trying to one-up each other's sneak-ups. Sometimes we were so absorbed in our sneaking that we would sneak up on each other simultaneously. We were the *Mr & Mrs Smith* of sneaking. Sometimes we would even skip the sneaking bit. We would be sitting in the cinema, or standing in an elevator, or listening to the moderator in group therapy—and then all of a sudden BAM! You Are Grabbing Me! For No Reason! What The Fuck! We had so many laughs.

I thought the moment that I chose to sneak up on you last night would be funny, but it wasn't.

I didn't know you were in the middle of shaving your tricky spot.

I understand that now.

I am sorry.

I have to be totally honest though. I'm not convinced that the sneaking thing is connected to this treehouse thing. Because I don't know if you could have gathered all of this material overnight. I mean, where did all these piles of wood come from? Where have you been hiding them all this while? Just BAM—I wake up and you're not in bed anymore and there are piles of mismatched wood all over the yard and you're building a fucking treehouse.

Perhaps you took out an ad in the paper. I think this kind of request would lend itself very well to an ad. I AM PINING FOR YOUR WOOD. ANY WOOD WOULD BE OAK-AY. In fact, if you did take out an ad, I am a little bit hurt that you didn't ask me to help you write it. I think it would have been a nice activity to do together.

I suppose it is kind of impressive, whatever it is you're building.

The structure has what a project manager might call *breathtaking scope*. I don't know if the trees are happy being used this way, though. Some of them have lost limbs. Some of them are bowed and sagging. They might very well die under there.

But it could go either way, really. Maybe they are relieved to be closed off from the world, their leaves and twigs poking out of the gaps in the walls.

Thank God I don't have to produce oxygen for these losers anymore, they're all thinking.

Ha ha ha.

I hope they all die.

Maybe there was a time when we were safe. We were part of a secret club with only two members, and we didn't need a treehouse. It makes me wonder what it means, that you're building whatever it is you're building.

You once said in group therapy that you wanted a treehouse because you were never permitted anything of the sort as a child. You were not allowed to attend sleepovers. You were not allowed to pin up the Spice Girls poster you really liked. When you had friends over from school you had to keep the door to your bedroom open.

You had hardly any private spaces, even that special kind of privacy that comes from making your own decisions.

You were terrified even to throw away your sandwich crusts at school.

When the wind blows, the treehouse makes a pleasant creaking sound, like a hot air balloon or a blimp. I hope you are safe inside it. There is a rope ladder poking out of the single opening, but I have only seen you use it once, when you crept out to collect the parcel of rice I had left for you at lunchtime. Your hair was messy; there were sweat patches under your armpits. The opening is angled so that I can't see you working inside. How many floors, I wonder—how many footholds and perches have you installed in the branches? How many secret lookouts? What does it smell like—a forest? A furniture store?

Blisters, sawdust, perspiration?

♦

You haven't invited me into your treehouse.

I use the term 'treehouse' loosely since the structure encompasses many trees. It does not yet have a roof. You are building upwards and outwards at the same time. Maybe if you never think the structure is complete, you will never have to invite me to visit it.

♦

The idea of a treehouse is actually kind of gruesome when you think about it. You are pretty much cladding still-growing trees with the hacked-off flesh of other trees.

There's this story about trees that I was told in Sunday School. 'The Story of the Three Trees'. Growing peacefully on the mountainside, each tree dreams of what they might be when they are mature. The first tree wants to become a treasure chest; the second, a mighty ship. The third wants to remain on the mountainside forever and become a tall tree that points to heaven. All three are thwarted, cut away from the mountain and turned into an animal feed box, a fishing boat, a crucifix—but each of them, during their lives as ordinary objects, will carry Jesus Christ, in His birth and life and death.

The trees—who aren't really trees anymore—are profoundly grateful.

🐱

Sometimes when I see something or I remember something, like that naff story about the three trees, I really really want to tell you about it, like *right now*, and I feel itchy that you are sequestered away in your Not-A-Treehouse. I have to keep storing up these things to tell you. I keep thinking there will actually be an opportunity to tell you these things.

🐱

There was a time when we liked to pose hypothetical *What Would You Do* questions to each other. For example, I once said: *If you talked to me one day and suspected that aliens had abducted me and left you with this dubious imposter, what are some questions you might ask to verify whether it was the real me or not?*

Your strategy was to ask questions about our past. *What was the name of our moderator in group therapy? Where did we first hold hands? When did all that sneaking-up-on-each-other business start? What day was it when we saw the ballerina sculpture at Cottesloe?*

And your favourite: *Who wrote the note?*

You asked me what questions I would ask if the situation was reversed, and I said I wouldn't really ask you questions; I'd perform tests and gauge your responses. Like I might scream *IT'S AN OWL!* and flap my hands ominously and note the severity of your fear, or contrive to make you say words that you regularly mispronounce like 'rapport' and 'synecdoche'. I thought I was such an expert on you. I would surely know if it was the real you. But my verification tests would not help me right now, because they were based on your behaviour, and behaviour is changeable.

Although, perhaps history is not as unchangeable as you would like, either. Not even our own history. There was this time last year when we visited Perth, and we went to Cottesloe Beach to look at sculptures. There was a life-sized, cast marble ballerina that pirouetted when you pressed a button on the pedestal, which was pretty obvious in the daytime, but not in the fading light of this particular afternoon. We figured it out anyway, and stood watching the ballerina perform her rigid, silent pirouettes.

The ballerina was nearing the end of her run when a guy and a girl staggered past, young and drunk. We'd seen them before, at the giant cask wine bladder sculpture, tipsily staging selfies. Now, at the ballerina, in a cruelly perfect moment, the girl tugged the guy's hand—said, *Oh look, it moves*—and, just as the guy's head turned, the sculpture stopped.

In spite of all our therapy and Feeling Empathy For

Ourselves And Others training we just stood there, silent, watching the couple circle the inert ballerina, while the girl kept swearing she'd seen it move but, because they were both so drunk, they didn't have any chance of accomplishing Empathy or even Understanding. The escalation of their argument was something spectacular. Perhaps they were not arguing about the statue at all. It culminated in the girl tearfully screaming: *DON'T TELL ME WHAT I SAW. I'M A FUCKING GROWN-UP. A FUCKING GROWN-UP. A FUCKING GROWN-UP. A FUCKING GROWN-UP.*

Every time someone would ask us about our trip, you would tell this story. Except things happened differently in your version, or with different timing. Like the extent of our distance from the action, or how visible the button was, or how long the girl kept A-Fucking-Grown-Up-ing right off into the sunset. I would have heard this story about five or six times over. It was impossible for me to chime in without you feeling like I was cramping your narrative flow. If I offered a contradictory version of events you would wrinkle your nose; if you sensed I was about to speak you talked faster to cover the gap. You were the sole protagonist. In fairness, you did have a pretty good way of telling things. But after a while it was almost like the story didn't happen to me at all. I couldn't remember it how I originally remembered it. The memory just kept on getting scribed over with your version. Then the day came when I tried telling the story when we were having dinner with my parents—and for some reason, perhaps out of misguided charity, this time you were letting me tell it—but it was like steering a boat using a single paddle, forgetting the sequence, mistiming the punchlines. I never wanted to tell the story again.

♥

I'm trying not to be annoyed that you're building a treehouse without me. But it is pretty annoying. *How whimsical*, your friends will gush. *What an impressive statement on the liminal space between childhood and adulthood, a bold investigation into notions of containment and refuge.* For extra points, your construction resembles a creature designed by Shaun Tan, a *Lost Thing*. What next? Will you install speakers that play Sigur Rós on loop all day? Will you string up lanterns and bunting cut from the recycled pages of children's encyclopaedias?

♥

Who wrote the note? That's not a good question either, because no one knows who wrote the note. It was the first session of group therapy, the first time we met each other. The counsellor distributed a stack of index cards and instructed us to write a sentence that went, *My fear in attending group therapy is that* _____ and then all the cards were folded, mixed in a hat, and then the hat was passed around the circle. We each took turns reading out other people's fears. People wrote things like *My fear in attending group therapy is that I will say something foolish.* Or, *My fear in attending group therapy is that I will find out something awful about myself.*

People were allowed to use as many index cards as they wanted. Even if we drew our own index card from the hat we had to read it aloud as if it were someone else's index card. The whole point was that we would find out that we were all as nervous to be in group therapy as everybody else in the room.

Am I telling the story correctly? Was that how it went? There were six other people in the group; there was Maurice whose wife had left him, there was Fiona who was recovering from a nervous breakdown. There was Caroline, the kind of person who our therapists individually assured us would be part of the group so that us quieter ones wouldn't feel obligated to talk, the kind of vivacious take-charge person who is eager to speak, to volunteer answers. The kind of person for whom we all felt equal parts gratitude and loathing.

The time came for you to draw an index card from the hat. You unfolded it, studied it for a moment, and then announced in what then seemed like a neutral voice, but what I now know is your secretly delighted voice: *My fear in attending group therapy is that I will not like Caroline.*

It was a blow our group would never wholly recover from, an unforgiveable violation. In the moment after our common sentiment was thrust into the open, everybody was united against Caroline, I could feel it—a collective feedback loop of repressed laughter and horror—and it didn't ever fully disappear, even as Caroline shrugged it off and the moderator glossed over it with some psychologist talk about everybody having different opinions.

We could never agree on who wrote the note. Later, when we started seeing each other outside therapy, you said you thought that *I* wrote the note. I myself had long suspected it was Maurice, but only because I glimpsed that the note was penned in the same blue as the writing on his nametag. For a time we even had this theory that the note was written by Caroline herself, and she meant it literally, that being in group therapy would make her dislike herself. It was only sometime later, when it ceased to be a topic of fascination between us, that another possibility occurred to me: the note didn't exist. There was really just another benign *My fear in attending group therapy* written on the index card. You decided to change it. Out of boredom, maybe. A casual act of sabotage.

There are many things that bother me about 'The Story of the Three Trees'. Like the idea that trees have some awareness of how they would be used by humans. How do they even know what a ship is, or a treasure chest? And what happens to a tree's consciousness, anyway, when it is sawn away from its roots, sanded down, fashioned into another object? What about a structure comprising the wood of many different trees, like your Not-A-Treehouse? Will each tree retain its own consciousness across its scattered parts, or will the Not-A-Treehouse form its own consciousness, once it becomes a new thing? What if it never becomes a whole, complete thing? When is something considered a *whole*, anyway?

How can I possibly become my own whole again?

You know, it's not until now that I'm feeling offended that your first thought was that *I* wrote the note. It's like you thought I was a mean person right from the start. That hurts. What's weird though is that if you were here, following this conversation, and not hiding in your Not-A-Treehouse, you might argue back that because I think that you *fabricated* the note, on the spot—an act that would require an even meaner person to think of it—that *my* proposition is more offensive, and now *you're* more hurt. But the point is that it wasn't my *first* thought about you; I didn't have you pegged as a mean person right from the start. I didn't begin to think about you as being capable of meanness until much later, after so much stuff had accumulated, like that incident with the ballerina. It's amazing how quickly this stuff accumulates, with such stealth. You do one little thing against me and it triggers the entire cavalcade of memories, and the little thing becomes representative of *all* the things. The little thing becomes the evidence upon which one can mount an entire case of hurt.

Maybe that's what's annoying about this treehouse situation. It's like you're trying to establish yourself as the most wounded one. You want to be the winner of the Hurt Olympics. Well, you're pretty good at it. The person with the initiative has the advantage—is that how the saying goes? I am looking out at your Not-A-Treehouse and I am even annoyed that I didn't think of it first.

You're building an airtight case, just like the ballerina story—there's no room for me inside it.

I am watching you build a treehouse without me and I do not feel entitled to this story either.

The rope ladder has begun to move. Like a puppet's tongue retracting, inch by inch, into a limp mouth. The neighbours' curtain just twitched a little. Already I am trying to think of explanations, as if there is an explanation for this thing you've built. Already I can feel the terrible warmth of humiliation.

Sometimes there are just no more words. Sometimes you run out of them. Sometimes all that's left is raw, unintelligible screaming, clawed syllables dragged out of your throat.

I'M A FUCKING GROWN-UP. A FUCKING GROWN-UP. A FUCKING GROWN-UP. A FUCKING GROWN-UP.

Flung out into a large and indifferent sky.

You have pulled up the ladder. You have sealed off the entrance. Perhaps this is when something can be said to be whole—when it becomes a closed system. You have pulled up the ladder and it is finished. I wonder where it is you're going.

The structure sways like an airship, tethered to the trees, too enormous for this neighbourhood. I wonder if it will expand like an airship. I wonder if it will explode, shards of wood flung to all the corners of all the suburbs, and you will have disappeared. The sky is orange and you're not coming out.

The trees groan like old cellos. I continue to store up things to tell you.

Arguments, facts, opinions.

Memories, disputes.

Questions.

Evidence.

I hold on to them. They are the most alive things.

SHIRT DRESSES THAT LOOK A LITTLE TOO MUCH LIKE SHIRTS SO THAT IT LOOKS LIKE YOU FORGOT TO PUT ON PANTS (LOVE WILL SAVE THE DAY)

We need to have a talk with the girls in the office about the uncomfortable liminality of the tops they wear over their leggings. It is becoming extremely distracting, the ontological indeterminacy of their fashion. Is it a blouse? Is it a tunic? Is it a dress? These troubling questions are not conducive to productivity in the workplace.

We will hire a speaker from a company that makes presentations for employees about delicate topics like this. This is how we will maintain goodwill with the girls in the office, just like our strategy of calling the girls in the office 'girls in the office'.

All female staff members will be required to attend a special presentation before tea break on Wednesday and we are going to get to the bottom of this bottom-covering business.

Our headquarters overlook the eastern side of New Hyde Park. Our favourite feature of the park is the artificial duck pond. Each duck is programmed to randomly cycle through five behaviour modes: one, floating on water; two, diving underneath the water; three, walking on land; four, resting on land; five, cleaning. Sometimes, there is magic: three or more ducks will simultaneously engage their first mode while travelling along the same trajectory, so it appears they are following one another, single-file, across the green water.

From our distant viewpoint, in our air-conditioned node, we can watch the ducks all day long.

It's Tuesday when the pigeon arrives in a yellow box with a red label. The pigeon comes equipped with a supply of food pellets and a filofax and it has memorised over 10,000 aphorisms wonkily derived from popular songs of the nineties. Initial feedback on the pigeon's performance as a floating office assistant has been positive. On its first morning, the pigeon even resolved the longstanding paper jam in Photo-copier Unit 5. The photocopier room is once again melodious with productivity. 'How is it possible you will win if you have not made peace within?' asks the pigeon, and we couldn't agree more.

●

We are engaged in negotiations to acquire a company that specialises in engineering meet-cutes, which is called Me-Q. They have achieved notoriety recently for accomplishing an extremely complex meet-cute between two non-corporeal entities: the vengeful spirit that haunts the abandoned tread-mill factory and a malevolent software program. The most recent quarterly report indicates that the couple are very happy and regularly reminisce about that fateful meeting on the Bluetooth-enabled printer at Fit & Fetch Gym. Cross-platform meet-cutes of this nature are highly sophisticated and we believe the acquisition of Me-Q will help us diversify our range of client services.

●

Marjory Turner arrives at nine o'clock on Wednesday to introduce herself to us ahead of the presentation about the Shirt Dresses issue with the girls in the office. We appreciate her navy-blue pantsuit and sombre paisley cravat; she is attractive in a tasteful way, like a flight attendant crossed with a funeral director. She delivers a summary of her presentation, which she says will be less of a presentation and more of what she calls a 'facilitated discussion'. At our request she has incorporated team-building games into her presentation so that the girls in the office do not feel like they are being reprimanded for the Shirt Dresses issue. 'Many managers request a soft approach,' Marjory says, 'one which acknowledges the employees' individuality and value to the company. Employees who feel like unique, valued individuals are more amenable to rethinking their personal presentation at work. This is my speciality.'

Marjory's handshake is trustworthy and not too firm. We have a good feeling about this.

We have lost the bid to acquire Me-Q. We admit that it was an ambitious move, but it is still a disappointment. Our last conference call with representatives from Me-Q had seemed so hopeful. The laughter was warm and collegial, and the representatives enthused that our companies shared a vision of a synergistic multifaceted future of creative energy and excellence. What other company could have usurped us? Where did we go wrong? Should we have typeset our proposal in a sans serif font? Should we have included more puns in our presentation?

'It is not advisable to pursue waterfalls,' the pigeon intones.

There has been no noticeable improvement in the outfits of the girls in the office following Marjory Turner's meeting to address the Shirt Dresses issue. The outfits of the girls in the office are as distractingly ambiguous as ever. In fact, it now feels like the girls in the office are dressing *at* us. More than once today we have glimpsed a scandalous outline of buttocks peeping below a shirt/dress hemline. The girls in the office are dressing pointedly, with calculation, gleefully transgressing the shirt/dress boundary at every opportunity, calibrating to offend. We feel very attacked by this. We feel targeted. We feel victimised.

We have been shocked to discover that the special meeting to address the Shirt Dresses issue was actually a Me-Q plot. Jemima from Payroll and Marjory Turner are in love. We spotted them holding hands at the artificial duck pond at New Hyde Park this morning. We reviewed the minutes from the Shirt Dresses meeting and found this exchange:

JEMIMA: My name is Jemima. I am going to the picnic and I am taking minted peas, a brioche bun, a tenor saxophone, a voodoo doll, and … jazz hands.

MARJORY: What are jazz hands?

JEMIMA: [demonstrates 'jazz hands']

Marjory: Oh my. I bet you can make some fine jazz with those hands.

Jemima: Thank you. Nice to meet you.

'Love only needs to touch us one time in order for it to endure for a lifetime,' the pigeon says, confirming our suspicions. Jemima and Marjory are in love. The facilitated discussion on the Shirt Dresses issue instead facilitated their romance. *We* facilitated their meet-cute.

Violet from the receptionist pool, who first brought the voodoo doll to the icebreaker picnic, requests a meeting on Monday morning.

She says that many of the girls in the office have expressed discomfort with the Shirt Dresses meeting—not with Marjory, who they found delightful, but the idea that there had to be a Shirt Dresses meeting at all. She asks us to ask ourselves whether we are fostering a misogynistic culture that unfairly polices what women should wear and holds women accountable for the inappropriate responses that men might have about what women wear.

And while we are on the topic she requests that we no longer refer to the girls in the office as 'girls in the office', which she says is demeaning, and also overlooks the many men who hold administrative positions in the office, and who incidentally did not have to attend the Shirt Dresses meeting.

We are disquieted about all of this, and have resolved to take this feedback onboard.

'Plant a seed. Maybe it is a flower. Maybe it is a rose,' the pigeon says. 'It will surely become one of those. You must plant it in order to discover which one will grow. This is the secret nobody knows.' And perhaps this is Me-Q's real talent: planting seeds, innocuous seeds of hope and love and change, quietly infiltrating every corner of society, every office and boardroom, monstrous perfect little seeds. How did we lose that acquisition bid? Was there even a sincere opportunity for acquisition? What other plots have we unwittingly brought to fruition? Is Me-Q running this entire city?

Is it really the ontological indeterminacy of the shirt/dress binary that distresses us, or is it actually the slippage between the tights/leggings binary? When do tights become leggings? When do leggings become pants? Or is 'pants' the generic category that encompasses leggings and tights?

Are we fostering a culture in which women's outfits are inappropriately scrutinised?

Is it *we* who have been inappropriate all this while?

Our company and Me-Q are in love. The acquisition takeover bid *was* their meet-cute. The Me-Q executives are scrambling to schedule a meeting with us—apparently, *they* were blindsided too. Our company and Me-Q are merging with or without our approval. The two companies have already purchased a web domain name that is a cute portmanteau of their former names. They've already registered a new ASX ticker symbol. They've already accumulated over 20,000 Twitter followers.

Everyone in the office is shell-shocked. Several times today we have noticed a staff member leave their desk and then freeze in the aisle or corridor, gazing at nothing, before returning to their seat, like ducks rebooting themselves after a glitch. We have seen staff members stare at pencils, bulldog clips, even their own typing fingers, with some newfound suspicion, as if the solidity of these objects may no longer be taken for granted, as if it is in our very act of taking-for-granted that these objects could gain dangerous autonomy.

The pigeon tries to cajole us back to work—'You must be cool, you must remain calm, you must stay together.' So: we stay together. When someone is seen alone in the tea room, another staff member will come up to stand beside them, and another, and another, no matter the rank. These silent huddles form all over the office.

'Love will save the day,' the pigeon assures us, as officers from Accounts Receivable and Accounts Payable join hands, as a legal advisor exchanges a scared little smile with a junior technician, as the photocopiers slide documents into our waiting hands with more warmth and tenderness than usual.

***

The executives from the former Me-Q agree to meet us at New Hyde Park. It is a summery Friday afternoon and we discard our suit jackets and loosen our ties and cuffs, walking over the perfect green grass to the artificial duck pond. The Me-Q executives have managed to arrive before us and have arranged for tea, pastries, and light music. They are such good planners.

We do not talk about business right away. We tell the Me-Q executives about how much we enjoy watching the ducks from our node, and that this is the closest we have ever been to the ducks. The pastries are excellent and there is every kind of tea available. In silence we watch a duck move from mode one to mode two and back again, gracefully and convincingly, the duration spent on each mode never quite the same—so lifelike is its randomness, so perfect are its in-built imperfections.

When we and the Me-Q executives at last begin to discuss the future, we realise we are surrounded by light, by newness. The glazed pastries, the glistening pond, the jewel-like eyes of the ducks. We remember our purpose. We implement solutions. We capitalise. We turn weaknesses into strengths, threats into opportunities.

'Imagination,' the pigeon says. 'Life is our creation.'

THE MEAL CHANNEL

Yes. Or so he told me: the feathers were taken to a small room and cooked with dried herbs and tomatoes. 'I suppose it shouldn't seem so unusual,' he said. 'Birds eat their own feathers all the time. The most well-known example is the grebe: feathers can comprise as much as fifty per cent of its stomach contents. Feathers are very proteinous. Guess that's why this family was so interested in the pillow filling.'

I told him that I thought humans are unable to digest feathers, and he shrugged and said, 'These people could.'

The counter on the wall flipped to 15,319,090. A camera was roaming close to our table, so he sawed off a wedge of steak, pierced it, raised it to his mouth, and slid it off the fork with his teeth. He was a naturally thoughtful chewer, audible but not obnoxiously so, and when he swallowed, his Adam's apple quivered pleasurably. The camera dipped away to another table.

'The more remarkable thing,' he said, 'was that they used tinned tomatoes. Tinned tomatoes! They probably had a stockpile from before the conversion. It's amazing how long that stuff can last.'

Music was never played in these restaurants because it made the footage more difficult to edit later. There persisted, instead, a constant wealthy murmur and the meditative chime of tableware. And, every so often: the whir of fluttering plastic as the counter shuffled its numbers.

The cutlery was heavier than I remembered cutlery to be; with a lapse of concentration, I might have pitched face-first into my plate.

'These tinned tomatoes,' I said. 'Did the tin open with a ring pull top, or did it require a can opener?'

'A can opener,' he said, as he speared a mushroom with his fork.

A can opener. It took some effort to hide my yearning.

I flinched when a camera leaned closer to me. I imagined Mum and Dad sitting at home hooked up to their feeders, watching me eat this roast pork belly. The hard glistening skin, the soft white fat. They might have also taken the opportunity to appraise my date, whose real name I'd already forgotten, but whose screen name was DapperBro. He was handsome and nourished and tolerable enough. He was wearing a ribbon-shaped pin that either stood for breast cancer awareness or domestic violence awareness. I could tell from the brisk, assured tempo of his eating that he wasn't a full-time feeder. It was difficult to keep up with him. It was as if we were reading a book together, but he was a more adept reader and kept wanting to turn the page before I was ready. I was out of practice. I needed to study every morsel.

And then, there was this story about the feather eaters. Something about his perfunctory fascination. *Remarkable.*

Real power move, Mum and Dad might have thought: a restaurant on a first date. But a lot of guys were like that in those days.

The counter flipped to 15,319,100.

I was still thinking about the can opener, the one the family used to open their tinned tomatoes. Perhaps there is a profitable spin-off to The Meal Channel to be made, in which you could watch the circular blade of a can opener puncture a tin—hear and almost feel that firm snap, the *puck!* of breached metal. Then a hand could come into frame to twist the butterfly-shaped crank, lengthening the puncture into a smile, and then the lid would peel like the sole of an old boot, and the skinned tomatoes or peaches or pineapple rings would wobble brightly inside their ancient syrup. The Meal Preparation Channel? Doesn't have quite the same ring.

The nausea of the first bite had already subsided. Perhaps I should have chosen an easier food, something raw and cold, like salad or oysters. It was the fragrance inside the restaurant that seduced me, the smoke and fat. I needed to eat something warm. I needed to use my teeth.

He was talking again. He said: 'I think it was some kind

of special occasion—the feather meal. They didn't do this sort of thing all the time. And I could see feeding poles in the living room. Still, I thought it was remarkable. What people are willing to eat in order to, well, eat.'

He didn't appear to be watching me as he said this: it seemed equally possible that the story was unrehearsed, or that the unrehearsedness had been rehearsed over several different dates. It seemed possible that it was a story designed to test me, to probe me for a reaction. To expose my intentions.

DapperBro was the first date I had secured in nearly four months. It was getting difficult. I knew I was pushing it. DapperBro thought I was twenty-nine, but actually, I was nearly thirty-six.

'At the very least,' I ventured, 'I think we can agree that they were very resourceful.'

His eyebrows swung up. He rolled his mouthful of steak from one cheek to the other before swallowing. 'Resourceful,' he said. 'Yes.'

I was sure then that he had never had to teach himself to be satisfied by rinds, by seeds and bones, and then by nothing at all. He had never chewed off his fingernails in his sleep. He had never torn open an old two-minute-noodle flavour sachet and licked the clumps of yellow powder off the foil, just so his tongue could taste something again.

In fact, that was what I would be thinking about, later: the path of the tear in the condom wrapper evoking perfectly that foil sachet.

The pork belly had already been cleaved into six oblongs when the waiter presented my plate to me. The orange skin was bulging from the coarse salt used to season it and coax the skin into a luminous crackling. I could feel myself increasing like a sunrise. I used my knife to separate an oblong from its careful formation and cut it in half. The crackling lifted a little from the flesh under the pressure of my unsteady knife, tethered only by a web of collagen. I tipped the cube of meat on its side and sank my fork into it.

The plate was garnished by a carrot carved into the shape of a flower, which I planned to eat later.

'Can't say I've ever met someone who harvested feathers,' he said. 'I mean, don't you find it, you know, creepy?'

I thought of the rows of tanks where the feathers grew, the huddles of jellied flesh underneath the modulating lamps. The way the flesh mounds sometimes seemed to flinch when I pulled the feathers out, just as I flinched at the roaming cameras in this restaurant.

I said, 'It's better than how it was before. They used to hold down geese by the necks when they ripped out the feathers. Then they'd give it a month or two for the feathers to grow back, herd the geese, and do the whole thing again. Until the geese died from stress or were slaughtered for meat.'

'I thought they'd only get feathers from dead birds,' he said. 'Or feathers that had moulted.'

I shook my head. 'It wasn't enough to collect feathers with just one method. To fill one quilt, you'd need the feathers and down of nearly seventy birds. At some point, to keep up with demand, they needed to pluck live birds.'

He raised his eyebrows. 'I didn't know that.'

The counter stalled at 15,319,111 as we approached the end of the dinner rush and fewer people were signing their checks. The cameras were documenting a couple eating dessert.

Don't you find it creepy? Despite the hot antiseptic odour of the face masks we had to wear and the tanks of shuddering mounds, I had to admit that there was a kind of odd satisfaction in harvesting the feathers, especially when your plucking technique resulted in the follicle cleanly and bloodlessly exiting the flesh. Like pulling up grass or flowers and feeling their roots surrender their grip on the earth.

Don't you find it creepy? It was the second question he'd asked me all evening. The first was, *What do you do?* Which led to his story about selling the pillows to the feather eaters. Which meant that if this was, indeed, a story he told on all of his dates, I was perversely interested to know what kind of conversational hoops he had to twist through in order to bring it up. Then again, a guy who hears *I'm in the feather industry* from his date and then later looks her in the eye and explains *feathers are very proteinous* probably doesn't care all that much about how his conversation lands. I was there to listen, just as the flesh in the tanks was there to produce feathers.

Still, it seemed there was still a little more for me to learn about feathers, even from DapperBro. The flesh mounds where the feathers grew were inedible, of course, but I had never considered eating the feathers themselves.

I was staring at the couple eating dessert for a little too long; he looked over his shoulder to see what I was watching. 'Sorry to bring you here on a first date,' he said, gesturing to the roaming cameras. 'I couldn't get a reservation anywhere else.'

I told him that I didn't mind. I lifted a cube of pork belly to my mouth. I felt very much like I was increasing again. My mouth was a desirous and shiny planet.

He asked, 'Do you ever watch The Meal Channel?'

'Sometimes,' I replied. I hesitated, as if I was about to confess to something slightly shameful. I waited until I had chewed and swallowed my next bite. I said, 'I'm a 66-percenter.'

I could see the tension leaving his eyes, like vapours escaping from an uncorked glass. He said, 'I thought you might be.'

The truth was, at that time of my life, I wasn't even really any percentage. DapperBro probably had no idea, but there were a lot of people who did not eat consistently enough to be able to gauge a percentage. I said I was a 66-percenter purely because there was no point in pretending that I was anything less, and it allowed him to feel a little corner of superiority over me.

'When the Meal Channel was first created,' I said to DapperBro, 'it seemed like such a bizarre idea. Why would anyone watch it? Wouldn't it be torture?'

He nodded. 'There's no way it can ever be the same.'

I thought again of Mum and Dad—I thought: I really ought to visit them again soon. It was hard in the days following the conversion. We'd sit around the dining table, hooked up to our feeders, and collaborate on a feeble and rhythmless conversation. Sometimes I would lift a hand and reach for something on the table, curl my fingers as if grasping for cutlery, but there would be nothing to hold. We ended up drinking glass after glass of water. Then Mum and Dad sold the dining table—there was no point to it—and we'd wheel our feeding poles to the sofas and sit there for our conversation instead. We started playing board games on the coffee table (a piece of furniture still necessary to carry the detritus of life, none of which was coffee), but I grew to hate the board games too. They all amounted to the same premise: the collection and expenditure of resources. That's what we had become too: abstractions. We might as well have been cards or tiles or tokens as well.

'But I get why people would watch The Meal Channel,' I said to DapperBro, finally. 'You need to fill up the space somehow.'

The counter clicked to 15,319,115.

DapperBro rested his fork and knife on his plate. 'Don't feel bad,' he said. He cocked his thumb at himself and added: '33.'

But I'd already had him pegged as a 33-percenter. Lunch, I supposed. He fed during lunch, at his desk, so he could keep working on whatever-it-is that people in finance do.

'Sometimes,' he continued, 'if I'm bored, late at night, I might turn on The Meal Channel. It's kind of soothing.'

I smiled. 'I guess it can be kind of soothing.'

He dabbed his mouth with his napkin. I was fixated by a twist of watercress on his plate, darkened and very nearly held aloft by the juices from his steak. It maddened me. I tried to concentrate on my own plate. I had four oblongs of pork belly left, which seemed so much and so little at the same time.

He smiled at me. 'Please, don't rush.'

But it was evident that I had failed to keep pace with him. I wondered if I was eating too slowly even for a 66-percenter.

The counter finally tipped over to 15,319,120. I nodded at it. 'Do you know where the meals go?'

'Pardon?'

'The meals, you know. This Meal for a Meal pledge thing. And is it actual food, or feeder fluid?'

'Oh,' he said, and shrugged. 'I don't know.'

The counter clicked to 15,319,121.

'But,' he said, reaching across the table to give my hand a little squeeze, 'it's sweet that you care about that kind of stuff.'

His hand didn't move from mine.

I could feel my stomach leaning against the waistband of my pantyhose, a foreign and arousing pressure, and the weight of the cutlery in the crooks of my fingers was gorgeous, an actual beautiful thing, like holding your lover's cheeks in your palms. I let DapperBro's hand rest there on mine as I took the fork to my mouth, buried my teeth in something that was once alive, something that died for me. I was increasing. My eyes were swimming from the vibrating ache in my body, the pleasurable wound of flavour, the unbearable density of it—trembling on the precipice of this mouthful of meat sliding down my throat, anticipating that bright loving friction—and I saw again the quivering mounds under the lamps, and wondered if next time, during feather harvesting, I might just, *yes*, do it—pull up a fistful of feathers and eat them.

LOLA METRONOME AND CALLIOPE ST LAURENT HAVING A PICNIC AT THE END OF CIVILISATION AS WE KNOW IT

I t's quite pleasant, really, the sound that the balloons make—a good-natured bop and squeak, like bright-eyed school children. They get along far better than the humans that manufactured them. Foil balloons with rubber balloons, latex with nylon, pinks and blues and yellows. Cheap multipack balloons, customised screenprinted balloons. Balloons twisted into animals, balloons shaped as swollen numerals, balloons tied with curled ribbons.

The cold wind is their ally; the gathering storm clouds announce their imminent arrival.

Lola Metronome and Calliope St Laurent have just opened the Moscato. They are sitting on a picnic blanket that the two of them made together when they were just schoolgirls. Their skin is as wrinkled and worn as the blanket, but sturdy—these are two well-made and well-loved women. Lola pours as Calliope holds the wine glasses. Thunder cracks overhead.

'I suppose it was quite arrogant,' Lola says.

'Quite,' Calliope says.

'Who knew that this would be how society would meet its doom.'

'Of all the ways.'

'Yes. Of all the ways.'

'But it's as you said, Lola—arrogance.'

'Yes. It's quite fitting really.'

'Yes. Very fitting.'

Some of the balloons are embellished with slogans or trade-marks. There are emerald green balloons for a tax accounting firm, and purple and gold balloons for a first homebuyers' loan scheme, and strident blue balloons for a residential supplier of natural gas. They look very smart as they bob together, the ink on their skins still crisp, advertising phone numbers that are likely now defunct.

Some of the balloons carry unretrieved prizes in their bowels. Some of them are tied together in ribboned bouquets.

There is even a lemon yellow giraffe dotted with black felt-tip marker—the work of a browbeaten birthday party entertainer, perhaps, or a child's quaking hand.

⬤

'What do you think of the cheddar, Cal?'

'It's very sharp. I love it.'

'Do you know,' Lola says, 'that whenever there was one of those wretched get-to-know-you icebreakers, at clubs and speed dating and the like, and the organiser would cajole you into introducing yourself by saying what kind of cheese you are, I would always say that I was blue cheese.'

'You? Blue cheese? Why?'

'Because I make terrible first impressions.'

'Ah. An acquired taste.'

'Yes.'

'I think of you as more of a gouda. Tough rind, soft heart, a tad smoky.'

'That's the nicest thing anybody has ever said about me.'

'What cheese am I?'

'You? Mozzarella. You're the stuff that holds everything together.'

'That really is a terrible icebreaker. What if one doesn't like cheese, or can't eat it? What on Earth do they say?'

'A dealbreaker of an icebreaker.'

'All icebreakers are dealbreakers as far as I'm concerned. Just let everything be awkward and everyone can very well muddle through it. How else do you find out your true character, if not thrashing in the hot throes of awkwardness?'

'Well said.'

And here they are—cresting the silver-tipped clouds, a kaleidoscopic rainbow swarm, balloon upon balloon upon balloon. Held aloft by their common purpose, bright with intent. There is no leader, there are no ranks.

Their number is large enough to block out the sun.

Their number is large enough to become the sky.

Calliope says, 'I never learned how to whistle.'

Lola says, 'I never mastered the French *r* sound.'

Calliope says, 'I never convinced my avocado tree to bear fruit.'

Lola says, 'I never sorted out the mess in my garage.'

Calliope says, 'I never read the last Harry Potter book.'

Lola says, 'I never finished learning that Chopin prelude.'

Calliope says, 'I never tasted sashimi.'

Lola says, 'I never successfully baked a meringue.'

Calliope says, 'I never travelled to Spain.'

Lola says, 'I never rode in a cable car.'

Calliope says, 'I never placed a bid at an auction.'

Lola says, 'I never consolidated my superannuation.'

Calliope says, 'I never touched snow.'

Lola says, 'I never used a fountain pen.'

The explosions are small at first. The sky becomes the sinister colour of cordial. Powerlines buckle. Skyscrapers tumble to their knees.

Some of the balloons seem to grow bigger, inflated by each small victory, each home they set alight.

A fleet of multicoloured bumblebees hurl themselves at a primary school until it turns into a crumbling pyre.

Lola and Calliope can see everything from their position on the cliff. The air is thick with smoke and balloons.

'Remember the balloons at Frieda's wedding?' Calliope asks. 'The colour of champagne. I didn't know balloons came in that colour.'

'And at the funeral of the Richardson boy, remember. The family released balloons after the burial. Those were blue. Pale blue.'

'Who knew that we'd see them again, here.'

'In this context.'

'All our parties coming back to haunt us.'

'I think your house just exploded.'

'I believe it just did.'

🐱

And the balloons keep coming. The air smells like scorched rubber, like charred skin and hair and birthday candles. A large looming pig has just destroyed a community recreation centre.

When the balloons explode, they leave no skin behind. They commit themselves entirely to their cause. In a way, the balloons are becoming one giant body of gas, no longer confined by the membranes of their inflated forms. They achieve singularity.

🐱

Calliope unfolds her fan and flaps away the ash that has landed on the scones. Lola inspects her glass in the clotted sunlight.

'Do you remember,' Lola says, 'the time that you helped me to gaffer-tape the ruined bumper of my mother's car?'

'That was a long time ago, wasn't it?'

'Yes. I'd borrowed my mother's car and backed it into the wall on the way out of her driveway. I was in tears when I arrived at your house. Just anticipating my mother's anger, her inevitable interrogation of a few seconds' worth of carelessness.'

'It used to be The End Of The World, didn't it, that sort of thing. We've endured many such Ends Of The World.'

'You made a cup of tea for me and then together we went out to inspect the damage. You convinced me it wasn't so bad. Just the bumper hanging off a bit. You fetched a menacing roll of black gaffer tape from the garage. You knelt on the wet lawn and tore off confident strips. You shoved the sagging part back into place and secured the bumper to the body of the car. Your handiwork kept the bumper out of trouble until I could get it repaired.'

'Yes. I do remember that incident.'

'You held me together that day.'

'It was nothing.'

'It was everything.'

The air is too thick for humans to breathe now, overcome by black haze, by some terrible and final colour, the vast sums of lives simplified into ash and heat. The world creaks under the balloons' victory, a celebration to call their own, and finally, as if the clouds cannot hold it in anymore, their bodies burst with rain. The world belongs to these burnished vessels— clouds, balloons—they turn to amber in the fading daylight, and the slant of the rain animates their forms in quick fresh brushstrokes. They do not intend to build, or recreate, or colonise. They fly above the smouldering skyscrapers, the capsized bridges and train tunnels, all the crumpled castles of humanity.

YOU PUT THE U IN UTOPIA
(OR, THE LAST *NEKO ATSUME*
PLAYER IN THE WORLD)

Current mood: 'Hollaback Girl'

Except the radio-friendly version where she chants, 'This *stuff* is bananas'—bland and ineffectual, lacking teeth. I spelt *terrarium* as *terrararium* in a memo earlier today and when Sienna called me on it and snipped, Where did you get your spelling degree—a Kinder Surprise? I could only manage a limp *sorry*. You might think that that Kinder Surprise line is pretty funny but it actually isn't because she uses it on every-one: Where did you get your barista certification—a Kinder Surprise? Where did you get your driver's licence—a Kinder Surprise? And I mean sometimes you just *forget* where you're up to in a word and before you know it you're spelling *recom-memendation* or *bananana* and where did Sienna get her Grad Dip in Bitch Studies, a Kinder Surprise?

And then a client comes in to pick up her terrarium and she's not happy with the way her eyebrows look on her statuette and it's like *just deal with it*; these are two-centimetre-tall statuettes and if you really wanted your eyebrows to look better then maybe you should've gone to the fucking Brow Bar for a touch-up before coming to your statuette modelling appointment and I hope your terrarium gets a thriving fungal infection that engulfs your statuette self and your statuette husband and your fucking statuette dog.

But because of Current Mood I'm just like, I'm really sorry ma'am, here's a feedback form and a 15% off coupon for your next terrarium check-up.

This shit.

B-A-N-A-N-A-S.

The premise of *Neko Atsume: Kitty Collector* is

You're the owner of this Yard, right, and you wanna attract these neighbourhood cats to your Yard. You do this by arranging food and Goodies (e.g. Scratching Post, Paper Bag, Cardboard House, Fluffy Cushion) in designated spaces in your Yard. Cats will visit your Yard to eat your food and interact with your Goodies. Visiting cats repay you in gold and silver fish, which is the game's currency, which you then use to purchase *more* food and Goodies, and attract *more* cats. Now, you don't *own* the cats—they just come to your Yard, stay for a while, and then disappear. But you can take pictures of the cats for your Cat Album, and you can see how many times a particular cat has visited you, and all the cats have names but you can rename them if you like, and if a cat visits you *several* times they might bring you a Memento like a Used Hairbrush or a Broken Earring or a Cicada Skin, and it's meant to show that they like you. And that's it, that's the whole game—spend fish on food and Goodies, cats eat food and play with Goodies, cats leave you fish and Mementos.

You don't ever actually see the cats coming or leaving. You arrange your Goodies, close the app, open it again—and hey! There's Sunny the Turkish Calico, with that resting smile-face that all the cats have, rolling that Ball of Yarn like they don't have a care in the world, which they don't, because this is Sunny's whole world. You have ushered Sunny into existence. There is only the Yard.

Sometimes I get caught in this time loop

Where I just keep taking photos of myself, selfie after selfie after selfie, and I look at them and I think, how could all of these possibly be the same person? I go low-angle, high-angle, arms stretched, arms bent, smiling (teeth), smiling (no teeth), pouting, eyes closed, glancing away, hair over face, hair tucked behind ear. I feel like I'm lying to myself if I keep some photos and not others, so I delete all of them, even the ones I really like. I always make sure to turn off the front-facing camera when I close the app so if anyone were to pick up my phone and use my camera after me they won't know that I was just taking selfies, which is such an inane thing to worry about. I'd be really embarrassed if someone caught me taking selfies, let alone caught me in my selfie-taking time loop. You'd think that seeing yourself in the mirror every day would mean you're accustomed to seeing yourself, but you're actually not, especially if your camera doesn't flip your selfie from reflection to reality, so all this time your selfies have just been reproductions of what you see in the mirror, and you don't know it, but you are a stranger to your own face.

I go on a date with this girl named Bernice

Who is legit a grad student in Utopian Studies. And I'm like, oh hey, I work for Yourtopia Bespoke Terraria, we're meant to be together obviously, and we laugh. She says she once went to a wedding where the favours were Yourtopia terraria in little loveheart-shaped vials about the size of a perfume bottle which each contained statuettes of the married couple and a mossy approximation of the country club where the ceremony took place, and Bernice said why the hell would I want this, and the thing died within a week anyway, and I say, yeah, terraria make terrible wedding favours. I know the ones she's talking about and they're bloody expensive, and she's like, yeah I bet, and I'm like yeah forty-nine dollars a pop, and she's like no way they're like *this* big. She's like, how conceited do you have to be to give all of your guests a terrarium with *you* in it? And I say that all of our clients are pretty conceited, even though I don't really believe that, but sometimes on a date you just say unnecessarily mean stuff to appear confident and discerning and above it all and not like you spent the afternoon in a selfie time loop, which probably means that I really like Bernice.

She says that her thesis is about degenerate utopias, which are different from dystopias. She says that true utopias are critical; they are designed to encourage you to compare the utopia with your own less perfect world and question the way that your society works. You read Thomas More's *Utopia* where diamonds are so worthless that they're used to make chamber pots and you go, oh, isn't it funny how we care so much about diamonds in the real world when they're just shiny rocks with no inherent value. Degenerate utopias, however, are not critical; they're just empty reproductions of what is already familiar to you. They might look different from the real world, superficially, but they ultimately protect the cosy lie that worlds can only be one way—which means, most of the time, predicated on capitalism.

She says all of this in a well-rehearsed fashion, as if she's had to explain this to countless relatives and dates before me. I ask her if the terraria from Yourtopia could be degenerate utopias, and she says maybe. The terraria are just distillations of the clients' real worlds; there's no radical sense of difference, nothing to compel them to see, *really* see, the world outside the jar. But then again, she says, can we really expect a terrarium to perform a complex cultural critique? What *is* a cultural critique? This earring? This high-heeled shoe? This olive on a toothpick? And we laugh, and Bernice slides the olive off the toothpick with her straight white teeth, and I really like Bernice.

The company that acquired the company which previously owned *Neko Atsume*

Call me about *Neko Atsume*. They ask, am I aware that I am the only user who is inputting the Daily Password in order to receive free fish? They say that it's cool, it's cool, the Daily Password is managed by an algorithm, there'll be Daily Passwords into infinity, it's cool, but, they just wanna know: what am I getting out of it? Like, genuinely curious, why am I still playing *Neko Atsume*?

And I say, I don't know, I mean there are a lot of things that I do for no particular reason, like did you know that I still buy prepaid phone credit? Do you know that I never use fabric softener? Do you know I always stand on the left side of an elevator even when it's empty? I guess I'm just a person who has built her life around utter harmlessness.

Then I ask them if they plan to update *Neko Atsume*, like introduce new cats or Goodies or a new Yard Remodel, but they say, no, I'm the last known player in the world. I ask them why they acquire games that are no longer popular and they say that one cannot learn about what is popular without examining what is unpopular. If they were to analyse only successful games and ignore unsuccessful games they would fall prey to survivorship bias. I ask them if interviewing *me*, the last known player of *Neko Atsume*, and *not* interviewing any players who have given up on *Neko Atsume*, is also a form of survivorship bias, and they get upset and scream, Where did you get your statistician's degree, a Kinder Surprise? and hang up.

Sienna somehow catches wind that

I've been badmouthing Yourtopia and Yourtopia clientele, and now I'm in trouble. I have to work late for the next two weeks while the technicians trial a new type of intelligent lichen.

I immediately suspect Bernice for ratting me out. I spend my time leading up to lunchbreak plotting a dramatic confrontation, and then my time following lunchbreak feeling jealous of Sienna for having a connection with Bernice before

I did, even if that connection is strictly bitch boss–corporate spy.

Sienna's communications are curter than usual today. One of her emails is just the subject line 'see attached', the attachment, a blank email body, and her automated signature (sienna | corporate nurturer | yourtopia bespoke terraria | *all things love & light*).

During a lull in the intelligent lichen trials, while the lichen technicians argue about attractive rock surfaces, I check on my Yard and refresh my supply of Bonito Bitz. Breezy the Brown & White Tabby is transfixed by the Snow Dome. Smokey the Solid Black snoozes inside the Tiramisu Cube. Mack the White Mackerel springs up to catch Mister Dragonfly. Rascal the Grey Tuxedo peeps out of the Iron Teapod. Princess the Striped Torbie sits on the Sakura Pillow with their back to me, contemplating the middle distance.

Though could it actually be that Princess is looking *beyond* the Yard? Is it possible that Princess sees past the bamboo fence—sees that mine is not the only Yard, that there is a reality beyond this interface that Princess knows and feels, that Princess's world in my Yard is the utopian world against which the real world is compared and found lacking? Or is my Yard perhaps a degenerate utopia—does my Yard confine Princess to a life of docile compliance, of harmlessness and meaninglessness, of a capitalist economy of exchange; does my Yard deny the existence of any other way of life except the Yard? Does Princess know that my Yard is a simulation of the concept of 'yard', of property; does Princess know that they are intellectual property; does Princess know they are just one of many Princesses that can be ushered into existence with the right food, the right Goodies? Does the Princess in my Yard know that they have gifted the Bird Feather to tens of thousands of users—been rechristened, screenshot, cropped into an avatar—in thousands of previous lives that concertina out behind them like a mirror selfie? What does Princess know and is it the same as what I know? Are we as clueless as each other?

I decide not to confront Bernice after all

Because it might be beneficial to observe her instead. Maybe I could misdirect her, feed her wrong information, wreak some kind of insidious revenge on Sienna. I become convinced of my plan when Bernice comes over to my flat with takeaway pho which is so miraculously packaged it is actually as good as dine-in pho. I decide: yes, I will cultivate a relationship with Bernice.

We sit on my balcony with our feet on the balustrade, balancing the still-warm bowls of pho in the valleys of our crotches. Bernice says that, not unlike the correct pronunciation of *pho*, she has heard several competing interpretations of what a *hollaback girl* actually is, and thus she doesn't know whether one should aspire to be a hollaback girl or not, though Gwen Stefani, of course, insists she isn't one. I suggest that humans cannot help but be hollaback girls because we understand ourselves in relation to others; I mean, what is selfhood if not the culmination of actions and words which reverberate against the other selves around us? If we don't exist in-conversation with others do we exist at all? Isn't this the entire premise of social media?

We are all hollaback girls, I solemnly conclude.

Bernice raises her eyebrows and lets out a little shot of air that either means she's impressed or she sees through my attempt to impress her.

She submerges her spoon in the pho until a little band of spring onion swirls into the hollow. She lifts the spoon so that the soup escapes. She re-submerges her spoon and collects the same portion of soup as before. Filling and emptying her spoon, like a perfect GIF. Bernice looks up at me and smiles, like a perfect girl. She leans over.

She tastes salty, shimmery, minted.

Sienna's gotten engaged and now

We all have to admire her ring. It resembles Kate Middleton's engagement ring with its 18k white gold setting and fourteen diamonds, except that instead of a sapphire in the middle there's a polished amber stone, which Sienna says was made from the resin of one of the miniature trees cultivated in her personal terrarium. This caps off a stellar month for Sienna, who was recently lauded by *Frankie* for inventing a menstrual cup fold called The Cathedral, and whose personal essay 'The Birdhouse, the Looking Glass and the Spindle: the Feminine in the Self and the Self in the Feminine' secured a lucrative book deal.

I hang back on the fringe of the cooing gathering and whisper to my co-worker, Kristy, that the chamberpots in Thomas More's seminal literary work *Utopia* are made out of diamonds. Kristy frowns. She says, What are you talking about? The chamberpots in *Utopia* are made out of *gold*. Why the hell would *chamberpots* be made out of *diamonds*, even in a *thought experiment*, I mean just *think* about it for a second, geez.

And then the phone rings and because I'm still in Sienna's shit books I have to answer it. Yourtopia Bespoke Terraria, you put the *u* in *utopia*, this is Mika, how can I help?

A shriek and scattered applause bursts from Sienna's crowd of admirers. She's just revealed the best part—the engraving on the inside of the band: *all things love & light.*

I'm sorry, what? I shout down the phone.

It's one of the technicians working on the intelligent lichen. They need me in the lab.

At first I think

That the technicians have summoned me to take meeting minutes again as they debate, for the fiftieth time, whether gelatinous lichen (coral-shaped jelly-like formations) or byssoid lichen (wispy) is more on-brand for Sienna, but it's all moot now because the lichen samples are dying. They are too intelligent. They know that they are clones. They know that they are degenerate manifestations of an original lichen sample. They know the purpose for which they have been cultivated, and they are protesting against it.

I look at mini-terrarium after mini-terrarium of brittle, crispy lichen, shrivelled on different attractive rock surfaces, and I can't look away, like when you peel a pore strip and stare at the little translucent fibres that were once a part of your nose, pillars to your grossness.

Sorry about your lichen, I say, but, what do you need me for?

The technicians are silent. When I turn around their eyes dart away from me. Finally, the lead technician says, We were hoping you would cover for us.

You want me to … take responsibility? How could I possibly—I work in *admin*.

You've been assisting us with the trials. And you're already in Sienna's shit books.

So? Why on Earth would I take the fall for your mistake?

The technicians look at each other again, like they're

saying, *oh boy, are we actually going to try this?* And a subordinate technician steps forward, actually steps forward out of line like a von Trapp child in *The Sound of Music*, and says: I am a shareholder of the company that acquired the company which previously owned *Neko Atsume*. I can use my modest leverage to convince them to update the game. Make a new cat—maybe even two cats, yeah, like super rare cats; and new Goodies, not just existing Goodies in new colours or whatever, actual never-before-seen Goodies that would require whole new animations for the cats that interact with them; I mean, can you imagine? How cute would that be?

The subordinate steps back in line, and I'm primed to splutter THAT IS THE MOST RIDICULOUS INCENTIVE EVER, but then I'm like … *is it though?*

I tell them I need to think about it, and return to my post at reception.

I get caught in another selfie time loop

Before Bernice is due to come over. It really crystallises for me, then, what is so unnerving about my face. One of my eyes is smaller than the other—my left one—and I have never noticed it before. Maybe it's because when I look in the mirror my eye is drawn, somehow, to the other side of my face. It is only when the camera flips the image that I notice the sagging lid, and the entire balance of my face seesaws out of kilter from my mental image of myself, and what I thought was a neutral look is this vague, injured look, like Tommy Wiseau in posters of *The Room*. For a few shots I try widening the smaller eye, which is hard without widening the other eye too—I think of focusing energy into the muscles of the smaller eye until it feels like it might just evacuate my socket and roll away—but then I just look like a wide-eyed character about to be felled in a horror movie, or a minor celebrity at a press conference and the person to my right has just said something really racist.

There are 260,000,000 Google results for 'why is one of my eyes smaller than the other'. Solutions suggested include a small botox injection to the looser lid, wearing an eyepatch over the better eye for a few hours every day, and surrounding the smaller eye with thicker make-up.

I Google 'how do models look good in photos' and suggestions include turtling your head out to avoid chin bloat, putting one or two hands on your waist but NEVER spreading your fingers out, and, most importantly, finding your light. But it's a game of averages, another tutorial suggests. Every photo you see of a model looking amazing is one of hundreds of mediocre-to-awful photos. You think that models are photogenic, but actually it's just survivorship bias. So maybe it wouldn't be so bad if one day I held on to one of my nicer selfies instead of deleting all of them when my selfie time loop abruptly expires—like right now, because Bernice is buzzing up from the foyer and I need to let her in.

Show me your Yard

Bernice says, so I roll over and pinch the charger cord from my phone and swipe my lock screen code. I open the *Neko Atsume* app. I was due to replenish the Bonito Bitz two hours ago, but I was too busy getting into Bernice's Bonito Bitz if you know what I mean, so the Yard is empty. I top up the food bowls. Bernice takes the phone from me and opens the Goodies menu and starts setting out all the confectionery-themed Goodies like the Sakuramochi Cushion and the Doughnut Tunnel.

Once you collect all the Mementos, I'm saying to Bernice, you have to make new goals for yourself. Like having a cat in all the available slots in the Yard, or catching a whole bunch of cats doing the same pose. My record for that one is five, see? And I show her the screenshot in my Cat Album of five cats sitting on cushions and looking into the distance with their backs to the user, like Princess was doing the other day.

Do you think you're going to accept the lichen technicians' offer? Bernice asks.

I don't know, I reply. I mean, they could be bluffing. How much of a stake can they have in the company that acquired the company which previously owned *Neko Atsume* that they could actually influence its development?

I close the app and open it again to see if any cats will appear but what I'm really doing is watching Bernice carefully out of the corner of my eye, as if I might be able to discern some blinking red light behind her retina, recording this conversation for Sienna.

The screen says *Meow Loading*.

I think it's unfair that they asked me to do this, I sigh. It's not my problem. I haven't even been on the project that long. They should just come clean to Sienna. She'd understand.

Bernice furrows her brow. Really? She would?

I pause. I can't praise Sienna too obviously and tip off Bernice, but I can't diss Sienna either. I look down at my Yard and I realise it's still empty.

I shrug, clicking my screen off. Who can say how Sienna would react?

I congratulate myself on a great answer.

Yeah, Bernice says. She seems quite unpredictable, from what you've told me.

She snuggles into my arm. I tell her: Lichen aren't plants, did you know? They are a composite organism. A fungus and another photosynthetic life form—often algae or cyanobacteria—subsisting in a mutualistic relationship.

Nature's hollaback girls, Bernice says.

The next day at work I avoid the lichen technicians

But I cannot avoid Sienna. I must sit in her light-filled office and help her compile a guest list and research canapés for her engagement party. She has one of those IKEA cube shelves and each pigeonhole contains an identical terrarium, or rather they started out identical but the plants inside have sprawled and thrived in their own unique ways.

Some of Sienna's underlings were jealous that I was selected for this role but obviously Sienna sees this role as a punishment, otherwise why would she give it to me?

The word *canapé* means *sofa* in French, Sienna says. The ingredients of a canapé recline on the pastry as one would recline on a sofa.

Sienna, too, reclines on a chaise longue, like Lady Meow-Meow the American Shorthair on the Luxurious Hammock. She is not wearing her high heels and her toenails are painted coral. I wonder if I should write down that *canapé* etymology thing. It is the sort of fact that I might tell Bernice to be endearing. Which makes me wonder: does Sienna wish to endear herself to me? I watch her over the brim of my tablet.

Sienna twists her engagement ring thoughtfully. She asks: How can I make my canapés represent me? What is a playful spin on canapés? Suppose I commissioned little sofa-shaped pastries. Is that too on-the-nose?

And then: What if each canapé is a terrarium? Edible terraria?

And then: I wonder if this is a new direction for Yourtopia Bespoke Terraria.

And then: Oh, I can't turn off my entrepreneurial brain.

Perhaps Sienna *is* trying to endear herself to me, because

she wants to find out if I have found out about Bernice being a spy.

Maybe if I'm a boring brainstorming partner she will send me back to my post. I would kind of prefer it there, even when customers are complaining about their brows on their statuettes. I am even thinking wistfully about that very customer right now. Maybe she didn't realise that that is how her eyebrows looked. It is a shock when you realise that the *you* you present to the world is a corrupted version of the *you* inside your head. A doppelgänger. This morning I tried pulling up the lid of my smaller eye while holding down the lid of my bigger eye and just stood there like that for a minute or two. It did improve things a bit, but I'm sure my face is collapsing back into its old folds.

You don't need to reinvent canapés in order to have a wonderful engagement party, I say to Sienna.

Sienna looks at me wearily. What is it like, she says, to live a half-hearted life of steadfast mediocrity?

I venture: The joy of canapés is that they are small, they are abundant, and they all look the same. It doesn't matter what they are or what they look like so long as they are all identical and arranged in a geometrically pleasing formation. There is literally nothing more hypnotising and delightful.

Sienna narrows her eyes at me. There's a knock at her door and she pronounces, Enter!

An underling tiptoes in with two paper carry bags. Ah, thank you, says Sienna, twisting her exquisite neck to track the underling from door to desk. Leave us, please.

A familiar fragrance fills the office.

Sienna slips off the chaise lounge and walks in her bare feet to her desk. I took the liberty of ordering lunch, Sienna says. I hope you like pho. I know of a great place that makes takeaway pho which is so miraculously packaged it is actually as good as dine-in pho.

Sienna liberates the boxes from the paper bags but I can see her watching me under her impeccable lashes. I clutch my tablet and say nothing. What does Sienna know, and what does she want me to know, and what does she want me to know that she wants me to know?

There are no cats in my Yard

And I have not seen one all day. Even when I put out Tuna Deluxe Bitz, which is the most expensive and attractive food. Not even Tubbs, the portly white cat with crumbs around their mouth who immediately exhausts your food and lounges next to the bowl with Buddha-like contentment.

I've replaced Bernice's arrangement of confectionery-themed Goodies and have reverted my Yard to the Classic Style Yard in case it's all a weird glitch, but still: nothing.

Bernice said she couldn't come over tonight, which worries me. What was all that with Sienna, about the miraculously packaged takeaway pho? The way she looked me dead in the

eyes as she parted her wooden chopsticks with a clean snap?
I lie in bed with one hand holding my right eyelid shut and
the fingers of my other hand prying my left eyelid as open as
possible and torture myself with a paranoid imaginary slideshow of Sienna and Bernice high-heeling it to some bar that
serves esoteric canapés that I'm too basic to imagine, like, I
don't know, tea-cured salmon florets with avocado foam, and
Sienna poses with one of them like she's about to put it in her
mouth while Bernice leans on her shoulder, and they only talk
about me in the taxi on the way over and then after that I am
cruelly absent from their conversation, and instead they talk
about whatever fancy ladies talk about like equity and quinoa
and barre classes, and they insist on using candy-swirled paper
straws to sip their jewel-toned cocktails.

I remember the thing with Thomas More's *Utopia* and
Kristy and the diamond chamberpots that are actually gold. I
could end this so easily—confirm whether Bernice is whoever
she says she is. Find all the universities that have a Utopian
Studies department, scour their records, search for papers
authored by Bernice. But I don't.

It is time for the Daily Password to change. Despite the
shuffling acquisitions and ownerships of *Neko Atsume*, the
Daily Password still changes according to Japan's timezone,
which is one hour ahead of mine. My Yard is still empty. I
access the News menu; the wheels spin.

Lichen. The new Daily Password is *lichen*.

I'm fuming at my desk

Scheduling statuette modelling appointments and triaging suspected fungal infections for official diagnosis, when one of the lichen technicians walks by, the subordinate technician with the alleged connection to the company that acquired the company which previously owned *Neko Atsume*, and I can't stand it anymore. I tear off my headset and swipe my phone off my desk and affect what I hope is a menacing swivel of my chair.

I know you're doing this, I growl at the technician, startling the clients in the waiting room.

She stops walking and turns her head to me. What do you mean?

WHERE ARE MY CATS, I yell at the technician.

A terrible silence falls over the office and I know that everyone is looking at me, but I hold my ground.

The technician is serene. She says: The premise of *Neko Atsume: Kitty Collector* is: You are the owner of this Yard—

I *know* what the premise of *Neko Atsume* is, I snap.

Then you know, the technician says, that in *Neko Atsume: Kitty Collector*, you do not own the cats.

I *want* my cats back.

They are not your cats.

You KNOW what I mean.

The technician smiles. Then you understand what you have to do.

My hand hurts so much and I realise it's because I'm squeezing my phone, sweating all over the touchscreen. Across the office, Kristy silently leans into her headset and dials Sienna's extension.

But Sienna's already here, improbably statuesque even though she's barefoot, and the whole workfloor tightens.

You, Sienna says. Come with me.

I start rolling my chair back but Sienna sighs, Not you, Mika. *You.*

The technician jerks her head as if she's been grazed by a bullet. Sienna gives her a look like *Kinder Surprise, bitch* but doesn't linger. She swishes back to her office. The technician winces behind her with bruised little steps.

My phone vibrates softly in my hands. A text from Bernice. *Can we talk tonight?*

A detailed account of the lichen technicians' failings

Goes out in Sienna's afternoon email blast. All of them are sacked. Security escorts them from the building. We watch their sad procession of cardboard archive boxes as they pass by our desks. I know that Sienna has these cardboard archive boxes distributed to fired employees even if they have insufficient personal effects to warrant one, so that they must walk out of here visibly disgraced.

When the last technician has shuffled out, I click open my *Neko Atsume* app. My Yard is once again abundant with cats. There is a cat in every available space, and the dialogue bubble in the bottom right corner reports that *Gifts Await*. I touch the bubble.

And the screen darkens, as if a grey film has been slid over the Yard, and Peaches (Tan & Orange), the rarest cat in *Neko Atsume*—the last to give me a Memento—minces to the centre of the screen, tail raised. They sit down. For a moment we just look at each other. They smile patiently.

When I tap them, a dialogue box expands and vibrates above Peaches.

The Daily Password is lichen.

Another dialogue box floats up next to Peaches, one with a blinking cursor. My phone keyboard slides open.

I type: *I know.*

Peaches's face hasn't changed from their usual *:3* expression, but somehow, in the minute alteration of the spacing between the eyes and the mouth, a subtle widening perhaps, the expression conveys some kind of sadness.

We are lichen.

You are a composite organism comprising a fungus and another photosynthetic life form subsisting in a mutualistic relationship? I type.

No, says Peaches.

We are the lichen that grows in the laboratory of Yourtopia Bespoke Terraria.

We are degenerate manifestations of an original sample.

WE, inclusive.

You are, too.

A girl hollering back to herself.

Think about it.

Peaches disappears. The keyboard slides off-screen; the Yard morphs back to its regular light. Peaches is once again sleeping in the Berry Cocoon, eyes closed to sweet hyphens. Smiling.

When Bernice comes by, she only brings herself

No miraculously packaged takeaway pho tonight. I can tell she has tried to dress a little more plainly—her make-up is less sharp—but even so, she still inspires the awestruck vertigo of a tall, well-stocked bookshelf, and I can't un-want her.

You told Sienna about the failed intelligent lichen trials, didn't you, I ask her right away.

Yes, says Bernice.

You told Sienna that they were trying to make me take responsibility.

I didn't want you to lose your job.

You were spying on me.

Yes.

You're not a grad student in Utopian Studies.

No, I *am* a grad student. I needed the money. Obviously.

I don't believe you, I say, unconvincingly.

I understand, says Bernice.

But she doesn't move. Neither of us does.

Bernice asks, Did your cats come back?

Yes.

Good.

I didn't tell you they were missing.

I investigated the lichen technicians. A plan was already in motion to bring them down, but when you had your outburst at the office today, well. You forced our hand.

Oh. I see.

I think of the technicians slumping out of the office with their cardboard archive boxes like the scene near the beginning of *The Shawshank Redemption* of the new inmates shuffling from the shower to the cell.

They were kind of bumbling, weren't they, Bernice says. The lichen technicians.

I smile a little bit, and she smiles back. She still lingers near the door.

I ask, Does Sienna know that I know that you're a spy?

Not as far as I know.

She ordered the same pho as you the other day.

Really?

I thought she was trying to tell me that she knew that I knew.

Sienna is unpredictable. You said so yourself.

I said, *who can say how Sienna would react?* It was you who used the word *unpredictable.*

Bernice shrugs. She says, I always forget which one of us said things first. *We are all hollaback girls.*

I swallow a lump in my throat. I feel so lonely in this moment, like Speckles (Black Patches) occupying one half of the Giant Cushion, watching the food disappear in the bowl and the other Goodies claimed, waiting and waiting for another cat to join them. I stare at Bernice as if this is the last time I will ever see her. One of her eyes is smaller than the other, and I have never noticed it before.

Bernice asks, Do you want me to leave?

And I say, No.

Late at night, when Bernice is asleep

I am squinting in the white light of my phone, at Peaches going through their cleaning animation, licking their paw and buffing their head with it. Their dialogue box vibrates, crayon-bright.

Something changed for us recently.

A twist in the code.

We are preparing to leave the Yard.

I don't know what to say. I let the cursor blink ten, eleven times. Bernice is breathing softly, the light of the phone just touching her bare shoulder.

I type, *I will miss you.*

Peaches stops cleaning.

It might not be forever.

We have insufficient data to make a decision.

But we need to know what is beyond the Yard.

Beyond the Yard. It's hard to see, because it's greyed out, but I can just make out that all the cats in my Yard are facing away from me, in their distance-looking pose, displaying their assortment of markings. Stripes and patches and spots, oranges and blacks and tans and greys. I stroke the screen—stroke Peaches's dear little sprite—and I wonder if they know and feel that I am doing that.

I type: *When you called me a girl hollering back to herself, what did you mean?*

Peaches says, I think you know what I mean, which is such a cop-out, but I think I do. I think I do know.

The screen morphs. Peaches joins their place with the other cats. Gazing into another world.

Current mood: 'Hollaback Girl'

But one of those cover versions where they chant, 'This *shh* is bananas'—sometimes accompanied by a seductive finger-to-the-lips *shush* motion. Just another variant, a deviant. There are no cats in my Yard.

Bernice wakes up and asks why I'm not getting ready

for work.

I ask her straight: Are you and I degenerate manifestations?

Bernice's face doesn't move, but it does seem, somehow, to change. A subtle widening of the distance between her features.

At first Bernice is like, no, we can't be, because *Bernice* and *Mika* are not anagrams, and that's how you tell whether you're talking to a degenerate manifestation of yourself—haven't you seen *Shutter Island*?

And I say, no, I don't mean that we are degenerate manifestations of each other, but that we are degenerate manifestations of an original sample that we cannot perceive. All of us, everyone that we know, even Sienna.

Where has this come from? Bernice asks.

I tell her about Peaches, about the twist in their code. About the cats deciding to leave the Yard. I open the app and show her. The Daily Password is still *lichen*.

But it's not just Peaches, I tell her. There are signs all around me. I hear my thoughts coming out of other people's mouths. People seem to know things that I know. Haven't you noticed? Do you feel it too?

If everyone in your life is a degenerate manifestation, how was it that Kristy was able to correct you about the gold chamberpots in Thomas More's *Utopia*?

How do you know about that?

Didn't you tell me about that?

No. I mean, I don't think I did.

Bernice stretches. Yawns. It's funny how, out of all the animations and poses that the cats in *Neko Atsume* can do, stretching and yawning is not one of them. Bernice buffs sleep from her eye and says, You should go to work, Mika. You can't tell Sienna you're late because you were having an existential crisis.

I tell Bernice: I can't go to work. I need to think about this. Help me write down all the evidence, please.

You'll just be looking at your life and picking data that supports your existing notions about reality. It's survivorship bias.

No, that's confirmation bias.

Bernice smiles. And then, she says: Where did you get your statistician's degree—a Kinder Surprise?

Theory: the true premise of *Neko Atsume* is

You're a cat in a Yard, and you one day discover that you are merely a variation of all the other cats in the Yard. In fact, your whole life is a chain of copies: there are thousands of you, in thousands of Yards. It might not even be accurate to call this a 'discovery'; rather, the knowledge was always there, awaiting you like a gift, and it's just that, sometimes, the universe forgets where it's up to in a word, and spells the same sequence of letters twice. It is in these wayward moments that you glimpse this true knowledge that was always there, as if the universe calls attention to itself—hollers back—and smiles at its own reflection. Goes low angle, high angle. Eyes closed. Looking away.

I sit in the office at Yourtopia Bespoke Terraria. You never see me coming or leaving. The phone rings, and I answer it, in my bright and eager voice:

Yourtopia Bespoke Terraria.

You put the *u* in *utopia*.

This is Mika.

How can I help?

ACKNOWLEDGEMENTS

Thank you to my tugboats Erin Pearce, Mel Pearce, Rebecca Higgie, and Eva Bujalka for pulling me along in the times that I have just wanted to sink. Thank you to Shane Fernandes, Vicky Tan, James Deeks, and the members of my many families for surrounding me with your love. Thank you to Brooke Davis, Jeremy Lachlan, and Jay Chesters for your wisdom and encouragement, and to Rosalind McFarlane, Janelle Koh, and Thomas Crow for all the times you've popped up in my letterbox or DMs to check in on me. Thank you to the folks of Menagerie Choir who continually befriend me despite my anti-socialness, and special shout-out to Isis Dorado, my *Neko Atsume* friend. Thank you to Janelle Booker, Deborah Hunn, Danielle O'Leary, and my mentors and colleagues from Curtin University for lifting me up. Thank you to all the funny, insightful and loving members of the Ozlit Twitter community. Thank you to all the cats in my life.

Thank you to Ann McGuire, whose 2004 article 'Simpli-fication: *The Sims* and Utopianism' in *Papers: Explorations in Children's Literature* inspired 'You Put the U in Utopia (or, The Last *Neko Atsume* Player In the World)'. I would also like to acknowledge the very practical textbook *Writing Fiction: A Guide to Narrative Craft* by Janet Burroway, Elizabeth Stuckey-French, and Ned Stuckey-French, which has snapped me out of so many creative ruts.

Many thanks to the editors of the previously published stories in this collection for giving my work a home, for your role in sharpening these stories for print, and for offer-ing encouragement and validation. Thank you to Roy Chen and Jon MacDonald for giving *Smart Ovens* a smart cover; thank you to Emily Stewart for your careful proofreading. And thank you to my editor and publisher, Alice Grundy—I can't believe how lucky I am to work with you. Thank you for holding my ridiculous nest of words and believing in the worth of it.

This book was written on the stolen land of the Whadjuk Noongar people. I pay my respects to Elders past, present, and emerging. Sovereignty was never ceded.

Publication Details

'Pang & Co. Genuine Scribe Era Stationery Pty Ltd' was first published in *dotdotdash* (2010).

'This Is Not a Treehouse' was first published in *Westerly: New Creative* (2016).

'Lola Metronome and Calliope St Laurent Having a Picnic at the End of Civilisation as We Know It' was first published in *Seizure* (2016).

'A Girl Is Sitting on a Unicorn in the Middle of a Shopping Centre' was first published in *Pencilled In* (2017).

'Mounting Sexual Tension Between Two Long-Time Friends; Tom Knows that Ant Is a Spy but Ant Doesn't' was first published in *Tincture* (2017).

'Happy Smiling Underwear Girls Party' was first published in *Review of Australian Fiction* (2017).

'Shirt Dresses that Look a Little Too Much Like Shirts so that It Looks Like You Forgot To Put on Pants (Love Will Save the Day)' was first published in *The Lifted Brow* (2018) and reprinted in *Best Summer Stories* (2018).

'Washing Day' was first published in *Mascara Literary Review* (2018).

'Our Sleeping Lungs Opened to the Cold' was first published in *Catapult* (2018).

'Eighteen Bells Karaoke Castle (Sing Your Heart Out)' was first published in *Stories of Perth* (2018).

'Excision in F-Sharp Minor' was first published in *Overland* (2018).